Born and brought up in Mangalore, SAURISH HEGDE is an MBBS graduate from Kasturba Medical College, Mangalore (Manipal University). A hobbyist filmmaker, he co-directed the short documentary *The Unequalled: Girl Child and the PNDT Act*, which was selected by numerous film festivals including the Pink City International Short Film Festival and the San Mauro Torineese International Film Festival.

An avid reader and blogger, he regularly publishes short stories on his blog. Some of his blog posts have been picked by blogging websites like Blogadda.com and Word Bite in their top weekly highlights. Saurish's love of travel has led to many exciting journeys across India, photographing distinct landscapes, which he shares through his social media handle @hegdesaurish.

Saurish is currently based in Mangalore.

Arjuna

the Greatest Lover

Saurish Hegde

Om Books International

First published in 2021 by

Om Books International

Corporate & Editorial Office
A-12, Sector 64, Noida 201 301
Uttar Pradesh, India
Phone: +91 120 477 4100
Email: editorial@ombooks.com
Website: www.ombooksinternational.com

Sales Office
107, Ansari Road, Darya Ganj,
New Delhi 110 002, India
Phone: +91 11 4000 9000
Fax: +91 11 2327 8091
Email: sales@ombooks.com
Website: www.ombooks.com

Disclaimer: This is a work of fiction. Names, characters, businesses, places, events and incidents are either the products of the author's imagination or used in a fictitious manner. Any resemblance to actual persons, living or dead, or actual events is purely coincidental.

ISBN: 978-93-91258-60-3

Printed in India

10 9 8 7 6 5 4 3 2 1

Contents

Prologue

A proud smile spread lit up his face as four women knelt before the lifeless body of the great warrior. A white, golden-bordered silk angavastram hung from the young man's right shoulder, floating in the wind. Even his white dhoti was pushed back by the gale. The light outlined his strong body, revealing a muscular chest and a pendant of Lord Vishnu firmly resting on the deep groove of his pecs. His right hand gripped his favourite bow made out of pure steel, which was flexible and taut enough to give the arrow enough velocity to pierce multiple bodies. The bow was decorated with many images of Lord Vishnu.

The war had taken place as a result of the Ashvamedha Yagna conducted by the great warrior. According to the rules of the Yagna, a horse would be set free to roam throughout the country as they trusted the horse to lead them to the next target. The person conducting the Yagna would attack the first kingdom the horse marched into. The great warrior had conducted the Yagna, the horse had reached the land of Manipur, and so a war took place between the great warrior and the young man. The result was an unsuccessful Aswamedha Yagna.

The four women were mourning their lost husband. Very little variation was seen in the attire of the women as all of them wore cream-coloured, full-sleeved blouses and white dhotis around their waists. Their eyes were filled with tears which eventually overflowed, smudging their skin. Their lips grew swollen from excessive crying. Tragedy had taken its toll on them. The sky was dark as the sun was hidden by clouds. The River Ganges was at her aggressive best, lashing along the banks, spilling water next to the lifeless body.

One of the wives couldn't contain her emotions any longer and she let her face fall on the chest of the great warrior. She was desperate for the comfort of her husband's chest. Then, she wrapped her arms around his body and let out a loud cry. The women stared motionlessly; the young man had achieved the impossible when his arrow punctured the heart of the greatest warrior to walk the battlefield. Now the title would be passed on.

"Master, you have achieved the impossible. Master, you have earned the right to be called the greatest warrior. You are the most powerful one, my king," the young man's faithful companion said.

The young man nodded in appreciation. He looked up at the sky, closed his eyes and took a deep breath. For a few seconds, he ignored the cries of the women and concentrated on the gushing sound of the River Ganges. Basking in glory, he stood next to the river, a feeling of accomplishment flooding his being.

One of the women interrupted him. "What have you done, son?" her voice quivered. Tears drained her of words before she could say more.

Engrossed in his victory, he had failed to recognise his mother's sadness.

"What happened, Mother? Why aren't you happy?" he asked when she recovered.

She stared at her son, eyes filling up with tears. "Son, why did you kill this great man? Today, you have made the biggest mistake of your life. He was a great warrior and a great man."

The young man didn't understand why his mother was crying for some warrior when she should be celebrating her son's achievement. He asked, "Mother, but you should be happy that today your son has earned his right as the greatest warrior. I have achieved what no one else could. Why would you mourn another man's death?"

"No, son, no, you have committed a great mistake, you have killed the person I love the most, the great warrior is my husband, your father...he was no ordinary man."

The young man couldn't believe what his mother had just said. It was a complete shock to his system. This young man was none other than Bhabruvahana, Arjuna's son with Chitrangada. He was so startled that his bow fell to the ground. He looked at the women weeping over his father's dead body. This was all the consequence of his actions. He had never met his father and had failed to recognise him.

The first woman who had fallen on Arjuna's chest was Draupadi and she was now crying on Subhadra's shoulder. Chitrangada joined them in mourning. Ulupi was mourning silently, a little distance away from them.

After a few minutes, Ulupi slowly walked to Chitrangada and knelt next to her. They looked at the muscular but lifeless body of Arjuna for a few minutes. They had both loved Arjuna and admired him. He had left the kingdom of Manipur and Chitrangada a long time ago when he was very young and was on a self-imposed exile from Indraprastha.

Chitrangada's love for him was never lost. She still loved him like before.

Ulupi felt sorry for Chitrangada. "Arjuna was a great man, a great warrior...but for us, he was a great lover," she said.

Chitrangada turned to Ulupi and nodded. It was true. He had treated all his wives with respect and dignity, and made them feel special.

"We should speak about the values he has bestowed upon us; we should recite the tales of his love and the kindness he showered upon us. We should tell his son how great a man his father was. We should tell him how his father had won us over with his love and his charm. Maybe then he will find peace," Ulupi said.

Chitrangada was convinced. She loved to talk about her beloved husband. Urvashi, who desired and loved Arjuna more than any of his wives, but had cursed him for rejecting her proposal a long time ago, stood teary-eyed near the wives. Such was the charm of the great Arjuna. No woman could forget him once she saw him. Urvashi joined the wives and they gathered around Arjuna, placed their hands on his body and started reciting the tales of the great man.

Bhabruvahana stared at the River Ganges as his father's tales tales of valour and love were being recited in the background.

Each of Arjuna's wives and lovers had a story they wanted to tell.

Draupadi

1

The Marriage

The Panchala court was all set to host the biggest event of the year. King Drupada had arranged the swayamvar for his daughter Draupadi. Kings, princes and warriors from all the powerful kingdoms let their guard down and competed for her. King Drupada was determined to find a son-in-law whose only motive was to keep Draupadi happy.

The Panchala court was slowly getting filled with participants. People from all over the country had gathered to find out who would be Drapaudi's husband. The court had a unique interior with a central pathway from the door leading directly to the chairs were King Drupada and his daughter would sit. The pathway was painted golden and the rest of the floor was pure white marble. The ceiling was decorated with various artistic motifs.

The commendable feature of the Panchala court was its huge seating capacity. The seating arrangement was at various layers. At the ground level, there were limited seats meant only for the important people and on this day, it was reserved for the participants. The upper seats were supported by pillars made specifically for this purpose. The rows of seats projected from the pillars to complete a semi-circle that extended to the other end of the court. There was a ladder that led to the seats from behind. The seats looked as if they were floating. It was a unique arrangement, the only one of its kind in the whole country.

The ceremony would start soon and the participants quickly made themselves comfortable. Through the door, a group of five Brahmins entered the court. Brahmins almost never participated in such ceremonies and they received a few curious glances from the audience. They sat at the far end of the court to avoid the limelight. The participants eagerly waited for the arrival of King and Draupadi. People took their time to settle down and only after that did the court bell ring twice, to announce the arrival of the King.

King Drupada slowly emerged from behind the curtains with Draupadi behind him. Everyone stood up to show their respect to the King. Drupada sat on his gold-plated chair. He had expected a large crowd but not to the extent that it would exceed the seating capacity of the court. He had no choice but to let them all compete. Despite the number of participants, he was worried that the task ahead of them was too far-fetched for any warrior. He knew that the person to win this had to be someone special. Skills were not going to be enough.

Draupadi sat next to her father. She wore a bright red blouse and dhoti along with a transparent angavastram. She looked stunning. Draupadi was considered to be the most beautiful woman in the country and men obsessed about her. She was the epitome of grace and beauty but little did they know how long she had waited to find true love.

"Today, I welcome you all to Panchala and thank you for coming to participate in my daughter's swayamvar. It's an honour and a privilege for me to have you here," King Drupada announced as people settled back in their seats.

There was huge applause from the crowd.

King Drupada looked at to his daughter and continued, "Let us not waste any more time in greetings and come straight to the rules of the swayamvar."

A huge bell was rung marking the beginning of the swayamvar.

King Drupada said, "The person has to lift the bow, tie the string and aim at the eye of fish right up there on the ceiling."

All heads turned to follow the King's finger.

"Anyone who is able to do it, anybody who completes this task will win my daughter's hand," the King declared.

There was a loud roar from the crowd again. The participants were surprised at how easy the task was. All of the camps spoke among themselves and were happy. Most of them considered themselves winners already in their heads.

"Now that everything is clear, let the swayamvar begin," King Drupada declared the contest open, eager to find his son-in-law.

A large bow was slowly rolled out to the centre by five men. Exactly above the bow, on the ceiling, there was some kind of mechanics going on. A fish was attached by a steel pin, which was in turn was attached to a horizontal metal strip that acted as the rotator. The whole thing was designed this way on purpose to make the task more difficult. The fish moved in a jerky manner, sideways, at an unpredictable rate. Only a true archer could dare hit the target.

But there was another level of difficulty. The archer had to aim at the eye not by looking at it directly but by taking aim by looking at its reflection in water. A small bowl of water was placed at the centre with drops regularly disturbing the stillness. The first participant stepped up to the centre. He was a young man and the Prince of one of the largest southern kingdoms.

The participants started mocking and insulting him, not considering him a worthy competitor. The young man didn't lose hope and went on to try. First, he had to tie the string. He held the string at one end and tried stretching it to meet the other end, but he had to bend the bow to do it. He tried multiple times, looked exhausted and his body convulsed due to fatigue. The bow didn't budge. The whole crowd laughed at him openly. The young man, humiliated and disoriented, was carried back to his seat. But it wasn't just the young man; the rest of the participants encountered the same fate. Soon the enormousness of this task was understood by all. The court fell silent. There was no laughter, silent truth prevailed.

Towards the end of the day's events came a huge, towering participant. He wore a light golden dhoti which perfectly suited his dark brown complexion. As he walked to the centre of the court, people admired his strong body. The man had a broad, muscular chest almost double the size of an average warrior. He had a perfect physique, a body tapered from his shoulders to his waist. His waist was slim and the muscles of his abdomen were clearly defined. He cunningly showboated as he walked by, flexing his huge biceps as he adjusted his dhoti. The girls at the stands blushed as they saw the perfect, bulging muscle and even Draupadi loved it. There was a prominent cross-shaped scar along the midline of his chest that told the story of a very intense battle. His long silky hair was let loose to shoulder level.

He wore a tight golden bracelet and thick armbands on both his hands. He was none other than the great Karna.

He had yearned to marry Draupadi for a very long time and this was his chance. The Kauravas had come to the court to support him. King Dhritarashtra and Karna's best friend Duryodhana were all there, watching him. Duryodhana and the Kauravas wanted Draupadi to marry Karna as it would help them strengthen their relationship with Panchala.

Karna stood at the centre and looked around. Anxiety had gripped the crowd. But confidence was radiating from him. As he performed, the court sensed the real possibility of a winner. Karna took the string, tied it to the lower end. Now came the hard part of bending the bow. With the string in his right hand, he pulled the bow down, exerting massive power. His veins bulged in his arms, his chest muscles completely contracted and his eyes were brick red. The bow slowly started to bend, and he was able to reach it with the string. He tied the string tightly and fixed it. The bow was ready. He had done it. Now he had to lift and aim at the fish. He was about to do it.

But before he even started to take aim, a sudden short bell rang. Karna was surprised. He looked up at King Drupada.

The man in charge of the swayamvar stood up and delivered a message.

"The Princess has an important message," he said.

There was a huge uproar.

"The participant has been disqualified and will no longer be allowed to contest for the Princess," the man said.

"But why, what wrong have I done?" Karna asked, surprised and confused.

"It has come to the Princess's knowledge that you belong to a lower caste, a son of a charioteer. And a queen of such high standing cannot let you participate in her swayamvar.

The Princess offers her apology for this but you have been disqualified. The protocol has to be followed," the man said.

Duryodhana rose up to fight for his friend, but the Kauravas stopped him even though they knew it was unfair. Karna's eyes were burning with anger; he was going to destroy her at the very next opportunity he got. His eyes said it all. But for now, he retreated. With all his anger he pushed the bow, and furiously walked back to his seat. With that push the bow almost fell to the ground.

Draupadi felt a little guilty about her decision, but she didn't want to marry him. It was her choice.

After the heated incident with Karna the swayamvar atmosphere started to gain momentum again. A few more participants were left to compete.

Then came the Brahmin's turn. He wore a simple long dhoti; the remaining cloth was draped around his shoulders. He had a healthy, lean physique with a thick mustache and beard. His rough hair was tied into a bun on top of his head. He stood up and folded his hands to greet the King and the Princess. Then he went on to do the impossible. He took the string, tugged at the lower end and effortlessly pulled the bow to tie the string. The crowd couldn't believe it! Wasting no time, he picked up the bow and pointed it at the fish. He looked at the water bowl and concentrated for a few seconds, then closed his eyes and set the target in his head. Keeping his eyes closed, he slowly pulled back the string and held it at the stretched position. It was an effortless display of skill.

There was absolute silence in the court, the anticipation was palpable. The Brahmin let the arrow fly. For a few seconds no one understood what had happened.

Then, suddenly, someone from the crowd shouted, "He hit the eye."

The horns and the congratulatory bells started sounding. Flowers were showered from all sides on the Brahmin. He had won the challenge; he was Draupadi's husband. The crowd immediately surrounded the Brahmin, everyone dancing and jumping around him. A pathway was made for King Drupada who was bringing his daughter towards the winner. The marriage was to be conducted then and there.

King Drupada hugged the Brahmin and handed Draupadi's hand to him. "Well done, you deserve my daughter. Take good care of her and love her till your last breath."

The Brahmin smiled and bent down to reach his father-in-law's feet.

Draupadi blushed at the sight of her new husband.

The marriage ceremony began smoothly and peacefully, but then as Arjuna was about to garland Draupadi, someone from the crowd shouted. Slowly, a group of people emerged and came forward. It was Duryodhana and Karna who were still upset with the outcome. How could a Brahmin prove to be stronger than the mighty Karna?

"This is totally unfair," Duryodhana said as he stood before King Drupada. "How can you allow this Brahmin to marry your daughter when you didn't let the Great Karna marry her? He was clearly about to complete the task," Duryodhana's furious voice echoed in the court.

King Drupada understood his anger, he deserved an explanation. "I understand your point, but you have to see this from our perspective and honour my daughter's wishes. If my daughter had objected to the Brahmin we would have disqualified him also, but she didn't. She chose him. I have to grant her wish and let her marry the person she wants. Besides, the swayamvar was only organised to find the greatest archer. It was always her choice that mattered," Drupada said.

"Well then, if this is your way of doing things, the unfair way, we will show you what we do to unjust people like you," Karna said, as he raised his giant gada.

The rest of the Kauravas also raised their weapons in unison.

Draupadi shielded herself behind Arjuna who firmly stood his ground. His companion Brahmins, the Pandavas, immediately joined him. A battle was going to break out in the monumental Panchal court. The crowd also took sides. A quarrel had started at the edges of the crowd, just when a dark man stepped in to calm the riot. He wore a dark blue dhoti, a wooden flute inserted into its side. In the small rope wound around his forehead, a single, elegant peacock feather stood out. He was none other than Lord Krishna. A companion to both the Pandavas and the Kauravas.

"Listen, people, calm down," Lord Krishna said. "There is no need for bloodshed in this beautiful court at this beautiful hour."

Everybody stopped and listened to him. Even the haughty Kauravas regarded Krishna highly and valued his words. Krishna was known to be an ambassador of peace, always preferring diplomatic tactics to bloodshed.

"I know it is hard on you," he said to the Kaurava group. "I know it is unfair, but I think all of you understand how hard life is. Each one of you have survived and overcome the difficulties and unfairness of life. So, I ask you to treat this as just one unfair act and move on. There is no need to punish other innocent people for what is in fact destiny. I am sure you will calm down and take the right decision."

He had indirectly praised the Kauravas for their ability to overcome difficulties. He had also taunted King Drupada and Draupadi for being unfair. His words transformed their emotional upheaval to conscious and logical understanding. He was the master peacemaker, delaying the inevitable battle between the Pandavas and the Kauravas for years with his tact.

The Kauravas realised that there was nothing to gain by fighting these Brahmins. Draupadi was already married and they accepted defeat. Duryodhana walked off, Karna stared at Draupadi for a few seconds, almost blurting out that a time would come when he would have his revenge. He too left in a huff followed by his people.

There were some murmurs among the crowd, but they settled down quickly.

"Let's continue the marriage," Krishna commanded.

King Drupada went ahead.

2

Draupadi, Wife of the Pandavas

The group of five Brahmins along with Draupadi walked past the village huts. At the centre of the group was Arjuna, who wore a white angavastram along his body, across his shoulders and tied at the waist to his dhoti. His long, rough unruly hair was tied into a bun at the top of his head. He also kept a thick beard and a thick mustache. He held Draupadi's hand.

Next to him was a giant Brahmin, who also wore the same attire as his companion. He was taller, broader, and more muscular than the rest. He didn't look like a Brahmin at all. His chest breadth was almost double that of any warrior, his abdomen big and round, but toned. His biceps were almost as big as the waists of the two similar-looking men beside him. He was the epitome of physical strength.

A little behind him were two other Brahmins, who looked smaller than the rest. They didn't have any facial hair and resembled boys in their adolescence. They were happily talking to each other and enjoying the walk through the village, and making a few comments about the girls staring at them. They were deciding who was better looking and which one of the girls to talk to later.

The last member was behind the whole group, as if he was protecting them and watching out for any danger. He seemed to be the eldest. He wasn't muscular, or athletic, or too young. He was just perfect. He had a well-maintained, but normal body. His hair was also let loose, but neatly combed back. He didn't have a beard but kept a thick mustache with its ends slightly curling up. The whole group didn't look like Brahmins.

They were the Panch Pandavas disguised as Brahmins. Before the swayamvar, they had just survived an accidental fire that broke out in the house where they were staying. The fire was a plot hatched by the Kauravas to kill the Pandavas. Luring the Pandavas to a house made out of wax, the Kauravas had laid a trap. Fortunately for the Pandavas, before the fire could be ignited, an informer had tipped them off and led them to safety through an underground tunnel.

The Pandavas had escaped and were hiding in the forest with their mother Kunti, when they heard of the swayamvar. After the swayamvar, they had decided to take Draupadi to meet Kunti.

* * *

Draupadi was clearly impressed by Arjuna's charm and archery skills. She took an immediate liking to the great warrior. Arjuna's arrow had not only pierced the fish's eyes but also her heart.

Draupadi wore the same attire as at her wedding; the bright pink sleeveless blouse and red dhoti minus the angavastram. She had left it out and this offered a glimpse of her toned, curvaceous abdomen. Her blouse revealed a generous amount of cleavage. She had light brown skin that glowed in the sun. She had a perfect figure and men from all over the country enshrined her in their wildest fantasies. She was well aware of the fact and thus had arranged for the swayamvar, to find the best archer and the best of men.

She had perfected a sultry gait, her hips swaying with each step. It drove men crazy. Yudhishthira was at the back of the group and had the best view of Draupadi's back and her swaying hips. It was a beautiful sight. Maybe that's why he had chosen to stay at the back of the group.

The Pandavas soon arrived at their hut. From the outside, it looked like an ordinary one. It was slightly taller than Bhim. Though made of sand, it was made hard by constant watering. The top of the hut was protected by leaves and branches of trees. It was built to protect the residents and the Pandavas were skilled architects with ample experience to their credit. This hut was good enough to shelter them for a few weeks. They would shift from there and move elsewhere soon.

They entered the hut through the narrow entrance, Arjuna and Draupadi in the lead. The interior was oval-shaped and much bigger than it seemed. It was cool inside because of the use of dry cow dung as flooring. There were two windows at each side of the room.

"Mother, Mother, please come out fast," Arjuna called out loudly. He was very excited to introduce his new wife to Kunti.

The other Pandavas stood behind the couple. They were not as excited as their brother. They didn't have a reason to be. They weren't married to the most beautiful woman on earth; she was married to their brother.

"Mother, I have won something, and I want you to see my prize. Please come here," Arjuna called out to her again.

Kunti was in the kitchen, busy preparing for the afternoon meal. She knew how much Bhim and the others liked to eat, so she was cooking the deer which they had hunted the day before.

"Mother, come and see what I have got," Arjuna insisted.

"Okay son, good. Please be patient," Kunti replied.

A few seconds later, another call from Arjuna.

No response.

Another shout from Arjuna.

This triggered Kunti's nerves and she yelled back, "Can't you just wait for a few minutes instead of bothering me like this?"

Arjuna fell silent.

A few seconds later, she replied again, "I have too much work to do in here, so carry on and make sure that you share the prize with your brothers."

Kunti was a woman of her word. She had taken a decision to live by her principles a long time ago. When she uttered anything, she lived by it. No questions asked. It made sense, it gave her a purpose. The Pandavas looked at each other. Was she serious or was it a mistake? Maybe it was a mistake, but Kunti had already given her word and Kunti always kept her word. Arjuna also stood silently, waiting for his mother to come out.

Kunti slowly walked out of the kitchen, wiping her forehead with her white cloth, which she slung on her shoulder during work to wipe her face. She was the wife of King Pandu and the Queen of Hastinapur but she had decided to live like a commoner and help her children after the tragic house of wax accident. She wore a simple light brown blouse and dhoti with an angavastram thrown across her shoulder. After wiping her face, she saw what Arjuna was talking about. She froze. Draupadi stood with Arjuna before her. The others were standing behind the couple.

Kunti realised that she had made a huge mistake. She had assumed Arjuna had won something materialistic. But she had already asked him to share it with his brothers. She looked at Arjuna tear-eyed and fearful, she was afraid she had done an injustice to her son.

"I'm sorry, my son, I have never spoken something and not followed my words, please forgive me for my mistake. I cannot take back the dreaded words which I have uttered." Slowly, tears started rolling down her cheeks. "Son, I have committed a grave mistake. I have not fulfilled my duties as your mother. I have ignored your cries, deeply hurt your feelings. Please forgive me son," she covered her face with the cloth.

"No, Mother. You may have uttered those words unknowingly but I have to honour your words. Mother, we brothers will happily share and keep Draupadi happy," he consoled her, but deep inside, he felt the pain. He had lost Draupadi. He knew that she loved him more than his brothers. He was the one who had won the swayamvar. He was her rightful husband, but destiny had other plans. Now he had to share his wife with his brothers.

The other brothers felt guilty about this decision, they knew it was unfair to Arjuna, but they had no choice in the matter. Also, they were getting a beautiful wife. So, there was not much resistance from them.

No one spoke for a few seconds. They were caught up in a flood of mixed emotions. Kunti was staring at the floor.

"Mother, it isn't your fault. Please don't blame yourself for this. We are happy to share a beautiful wife like

Draupadi. She deserves the love of more than one man," the Pandavas said.

At this very moment, Krishna walked in.

"Kunti, I have assessed the situation and all I have to say is, Draupadi was destined to be with the Pandavas," Krishna said. "Destiny has its own way of revealing things. Please calm down. It will all work out. In her previous life, Draupadi was an ascetic and she prayed for a long time for a husband. Lord Shiva granted her a boon. She asked for a husband who had the five qualities of the elements of earth and since there is no single man with all the qualities, she got the Pandavas, each representing a quality. Therefore Lord Shiva has fulfilled his promise."

Kunti regained her confidence when she heard this.

Krishna slowly pulled out a flute from his dhoti and started rotating it between his fingers. He had learnt this technique from continuous practice over the years. He placed his flute between his index and thumb finger, and flicked it, causing it to rotate around the index as the axis and land back at the exact same position. He didn't disrespect his instrument; it was just that he spent too much time with his flute and had learnt this trick subconsciously.

Draupadi had just found out that the Brahmins were the Pandavas, and the Brahmin who won the swayamvar, her husband, was Arjuna. He was her father's perfect pick and her dream husband, but now she couldn't enjoy her good fortune. However, after Krishna explained her past life to her, she slowly came to terms with the situation. She was okay with having five handsome husbands, it wasn't the worst thing. The trouble was that she couldn't spend as much time as she desired with Arjuna. They shared a special bond with each other.

Just then, another surprise visitor, Dhrishtadyumna, entered the hut. He was Draupadi's brother, and King Drupada's son. He had followed his sister to find out who the Brahmins were because no ordinary Brahmin could have completed the impossible task at the swayamvar. He entered with a broad smile in his face, touched Krishna's feet, and then, Kunti's. He bowed to all the Pandavas.

Standing alongside Krishna at the centre, opposite the Pandavas and Kunti, he announced, "I am glad that my sister will be marrying the Pandavas. Lord Shiva has certainly heard my sister's and my father's prayers, now I feel safe that my sister is under the loving care and protection of the Pandavas. Father will definitely be happy about this and I will make sure that the city of Panchala celebrates this."

Kunti was smiling now as were the Pandavas. Arjuna a little less. Draupadi was forcing a smile.

"Yes, we will celebrate but the Pandavas and Draupadi will leave to Hastinapur tomorrow and meet Dhritarashtra," Krishna said with a smile.

The Pandavas who were in hiding, after surviving the house of wax plot, didn't understand what Lord Krishna was suggesting.

Krishna continued in all seriousness. "Tomorrow you will announce your escape and your presence, approach King Dhritarashtra and rightfully ask for your share of the kingdom," he said. And this time your request will carry more weight because you will also be presenting Draupadi as your wife. Thus King Dhritarashtra will have to consider giving you a part of the kingdom. You are also the rightful heirs to the kingdom and he will do it."

The Pandavas were slowly beginning to understand Krishna's idea. Kunti acknowledged it with a regretful nod.

"Yes, Lord Krishna, we will leave for Hastinapur tomorrow. We will claim what is rightfully ours," Yudhishthira said firmly. There was no opposition to this. He was the decision maker.

The next day, the Pandavas left for Hastinapur with Draupadi in tow.

3

The Pandavas Return to Hastinapur

The arrival of the Pandavas was a grand event. King Dhritarashtra was shocked but impressed that his nephews were alive. They entered the court hall where all the elders were present. There was a huge round of applause for the family; the courtroom was decorated with the best flowers, bright-coloured clothes were hung everywhere with words of praise written on them to honour the Pandavas. The Pandavas touched the feet of all the elders and received their blessings. King Dhritarashtra expressed his happiness by distribution of meals to the entire kingdom of Hastinapur. Duryodhana and the Kauravas who were present at the court stood exposed. Their plot to burn their brothers in the house of wax had failed. They stood around silently.

Yudhishthira stepped forward and announced, "We have come here seeking for what is rightfully ours. Our share of the land. Our proposition is now strengthened by the fact that we, the Pandavas, are now married."

He held out his hand towards Draupadi, she came forward.

"This is Draupadi, wife of the Pandavas, daughter of King Drupada of Panchala."

Bhishma, the eldest, the most respected member of the Kuru family (comprising both the Pandavas and the Kauravas) was present in the crowd. This long-serving member of the Kings' dynasty was the mentor and supporter of the Pandavas. Since he was the grandfather of both the Pandavas and the Kauravas he always wanted the best for the Pandavas.

"I am very glad and relieved to see you standing here, no words can express my happiness at finding out you are alive," Bhishma said. "And you have just magnified my happiness by bringing Draupadi, the daughter of a close friend of mine to our family. I hope all of you live happily with her. This is the best news I have heard in a long time. May Lord Shiva bless you all."

The Pandavas folded their hands and bowed their heads respectfully.

"And yes, you will receive a part of the kingdom which is rightfully yours," he continued. "The Pandavas and the Kauravas are the same to me; both are capable and deserving of ruling an entire kingdom."

Just as he was about to say something more, Shakuni whispered something in the ear of the King. Shakuni was a close aid to the King and a closer friend to the Kauravas. He hated the Pandavas and never wanted to see them rule Hastinapur. A quick discussion led to Dhritarashtra's conclusion. It was decided that a peaceful settlement could only happen by co-existence and sharing.

"Yes, I will grant the Pandavas the northern half of the kingdom, Khandavaprastha and you Yudhishthira will be king there with Draupadi your Princess and your brothers. It seems like a fair offer," the King said.

The audience standing near the Kauravas started clapping. They were happy with the decision. They would get the better part of the deal.

Khandavaprastha was basically a wasteland, infertile and rendered totally useless. Shakuni had told King Dhritarashtra to give Pandavas the wasteland so that the Kauravas could rule Hastinapur. King Dhritarashtra didn't want a fight between his sons and the Pandavas, so he listened to Shakuni because he knew that the Pandavas would respect his decision even if he was completely wrong. They wouldn't go against their elders unlike the Kauravas who would fight for Hastinapur shamelessly.

Though Bhim and Arjuna were not happy with his decision, Yudhishthira smiled and bowed. Nakul and Sahadev didn't understand the complexity of the sharing arrangement and were happy if the others were content.

"Thank you, Uncle, with your blessings we can strive with commitment to make Khandavaprastha our home," Yudhishthira said politely.

King Dhritarashtra was pleased with Yudhishthira's reaction but he also knew that this was very unfair on his part. Even though he was the father of the Kauravas, he knew that eventually the Pandavas would win the kingdom through divine intervention.

4

Arjuna and Draupadi's Playful Night

An excited Arjuna ran through the forest trying to catch hold of Draupadi's angavastram. Draupadi and Arjuna were on a date. He chased after her playfully in the woods. They could only afford such quality time together because the others were at the conference hall discussing architecture. The Pandavas had already shifted to the wasteland of Khandavaprastha, and since there was no proper palace to accommodate them, Lord Krishna with the help of his architect friend Vishwakarma, had arranged for one of his buildings to be the temporary residence for the Pandavas, till the city was rebuilt.

Lord Krishna himself had asked Vishwakarma to rebuild Khandavaprastha, from what was mainly forest and infertile land to one of the well-planned cities of the country. In return, Vishwakarma would be immortalised with statues and buildings to his name. More than anything else, he wanted to help his friend Krishna. The rebuilding of the city was already underway.

There was a constant problem with the water supply in Khandavaprastha due to the pathetic plumbing system.

Even Draupadi had to go to a pond which was situated deep in the forest for her bath. So, she used the bath as her reason to escape to the woods with Arjuna. Draupadi giggled as she raced through the woods. Arjuna caught up with her and tugged at her angavastram. She gave him a naughty smile. Drops of rain descended on the couple. The huge canopy of trees protected them from most of the rain but a few drops fell on their skin. She looked up at the trees and felt the rain drops falling on her face. Arjuna drew her close and they kissed. Draupadi cried tears of joy. She wrapped her arms around him. They spent the rest of the night on the thick carpet of soft leaves and plants which made the perfect forest bed, cuddling. It was the best night of their lives.

The next day, Arjuna woke up alone in the forest. Draupadi had left. He remembered that he had to attend a meeting about the architectural plans of Khandavaprastha and rushed back to the palace. The meeting was at the hill top of Khandavaprastha. Krishna, Yudhishthira and Vishwakarma stood at the edge of the hill, each of them carrying a copy of the architectural plans, land layout and the demarcations which Vishwakarma had done. They were deep in conversation. They had come to a mutual agreement about clearing the forests for facilitating the construction of palaces and buildings. The major hindrance was that they had to relocate the settled tribes of Asuras and Nagas.

Bhim was standing alongside them but he didn't participate in the conversation. He wasn't the paperwork kind of person. He tackled all problems with his brutal physicality and sheer power. Even now, he was on the lookout for danger from the Nagas and Asuras nearby. He was always ready for war. Nakul and Sahadev weren't interested at all; they stood a few metres away, enjoying the cool breeze. Before them stretched the vast infertile land and forest. Khandavaprastha was much bigger than Hastinapur, almost double the size of Hastinapur, but the land was infertile and surrounded by the Asura-Naga inhabited forests. A strong breeze made Nakul's angavastram fly away to the sky. Sahadev laughed at this loudly. They were having a great time. Draupadi had also accompanied her husbands to the hill top.

"We need to burn down the forests, if we have to rebuild the area. I know it will be an expensive affair and there will be a lot of environmental after effects but it is the only way. We can plant trees once the construction is done," Vishwakarma suggested.

"Yes, we have to Yudhishthira. A wildfire will do. We can accommodate the Asuras and the Nagas further north. We have no choice," Krishna stressed on the last sentence. He knew Yudhishthira needed to be convinced.

Yudhishthira was a bit reluctant to burn down the forests, but there seemed to be no alternative. The Pandavas were meant to live in palaces and their cities were planned to be beautiful. Yudhishthira had to make a decision; it was a question of their integrity and standards. He agreed to it.

"Okay, then we will move forward with the project. Vishwakarma, we need to start the construction as soon as possible. And try and make this as safe as possible for the Asuras. Inform them about the wild fire so that they can leave the place safely," Yudhishthira said.

"We will try and begin this week itself; I'll gather my men here soon. Don't worry about it," Vishwakarma said, sticking to his reputation of completing his projects on time.

Just then Arjuna arrived, breathless from running.

"Oh, glad you could make it. It is such an honour for all of us to have you here, we are grateful that you have taken time from your busy schedule to be with us," Yudhishthira said, with his famous sarcastic smile.

Nakul and Sahadev giggled in the background. Bhim gave them a serious stare conjuring immediate silence.

Yudhishthira wanted to teach his brother a good lesson this time. "Well, what do you think of this, Arjuna? Should we proceed?" Yudhishthira's tone rose steadily. Yudhishthira was the most patient and tolerant person in the group but when it came to punctuality and behaviour, he always wanted his younger brothers to be perfectly disciplined. Yudhishthira tried his best to train his brothers when Kunti was not around.

"Ah, I think…" Arjuna muttered.

"Yes, what is your opinion about this? Tell us fast. We don't have all day," Yudhishthira was purposely pushing his brother to make a mistake. They had no work and plenty of time.

"Yudhishthira, I might have forgotten to pass on this message," Krishna intervened. "Arjuna had called me last night to inform you that he will be late since his headache persists. Clearly with all the duties bestowed upon me, I have let this one slip."

"You don't need to apologise, my Lord, I know you have a lot going on," Yudhishthira decided to pardon his brother. Krishna's words were final.

Yudhishthira ignored Arjuna and declared to Vishwakarma, "Let's start the work this week then. We need to make this area the best city in our kingdom."

"It will happen very soon. I guarantee it," Vishwakarma said with full confidence.

After a few minutes of sightseeing, the whole group led by Yudhishthira walked away from the spot.

Krishna had a smile on his lips. He slightly turned towards Arjuna and whispered, "Love is the final destination for all. I'm happy that you have found your love. Enjoy it. Great things can be achieved by love. Don't let it go." This was the first ever lesson Krishna taught his disciple, Arjuna.

Krishna walked away after this lesson. Arjuna spotted Draupadi standing near the slope. She had cleverly waited for everyone else to leave. Arjuna ran to her. On reaching the spot, he hugged her tightly and gave her a kiss on her cheek. Draupadi blushed. He held Draupadi tightly at her waist, both of them smiling at each other with their noses touching. The forest lay behind them and the cool wind caressed them. They stood like this for a few seconds and just when their lips were about to touch, Nakul entered the scene. Arjuna quickly released Draupadi, no matter how romantic he was, he could not do this before any of his brothers.

Nakul didn't realise anything. He simply delivered his message, "Brother, they are asking both of you to join us for breakfast in the hall. Please come."

"Yes, let's go," both said simultaneously.

Arjuna and Draupadi walked separately. They couldn't walk together without touching each other, so it was better to keep their distance.

5

The Reconstruction of Khandavaprastha

A wild fire was set in order to clear the forests. The consequences were serious and there was a lot of protest from the Nagas and the Asuras, but they couldn't do anything as they were illegally residing there. Yudhishthira had promised them houses once the recreation of the city was done, but they didn't want to leave the area because it contained the rich history of their tribes since the time of their ancestors.

Krishna had promised Yudhishthira the safety of these people. Most of the Nagas followed their longtime leader Takshak and relocated to the north, migrating in a huff and not accepting Yudhishthira's offer of land. The wildfire and the burning down of the forest caused a huge divide between the Nagas and the Pandavas. Takshak even vowed to take revenge on the Pandavas once he had an army. The Asuras were better than the Nagas when it came to adapting the situation because the Asuras were nomads who shifted from place to place continuously, so, they just had to pick up the pieces and move to a different spot.

There was one lone Asura who accepted Yudhishthira's invitation to stay in the reconstructed Khandavaprastha.

He was the architect, Maya. The wildfire had spread at a rapid, unexpected pace and this had made him panic. The Asuras were an organised community; their huts were arranged in a single vertical line stretching deep into the forest. So, the people at the end had some time to vacate their houses, but those who lived in the houses in front like Maya had to hurry. A warning was given by the Pandavas before setting the wildfire, but the fire, speeded up by the wind reached Maya's house before he could react. This was when Krishna had sent his men to save Maya and his family.

* * *

Krishna entered the house's palace hall along with Maya. The Asura wanted to personally thank the Pandavas and Krishna for saving his life. The hall was just a two-person wide corridor with wooden flooring. The hallway was decorated temporarily by Vishwakarma for the Pandavas. The furniture was all wood, not polished, dirty, and it gave the hall an antique look. The house had rooms for each of the Pandavas and one for Draupadi. Krishna mostly never slept and was always with Vishwakarma working out the plans. The labourers worked day and night.

It was lunch time when Krishna and Maya arrived and the Pandavas were seated in the semi-circle around the centre table. The table wasn't crafted or designed, it was just a huge semicircle log, the hard branches still attached to it and modified into seats. There were no utensils. The food was mostly vegetables and fruits from the forest. Bhim sometimes went hunting in the forest for food. Draupadi was serving food to Arjuna when Krishna and Maya entered. All of them were getting ready to eat.

Maya almost matched Bhim in size and structure. He wore a golden brown dhoti which was hand-made from plants. He also wore a matching angavastram across his shoulders. He had broad shoulders and a muscular chest. Each of the muscles of his abdomen was clearly demarcated, unlike Bhim who had a slightly protruding belly. Maya's biceps were admirable, but Bhim had bigger biceps and was larger and more powerful. Maya was an architect and he rarely fought any battles. The reason for his powerful physique was that he built all of his creations himself. He never handed out his work to his employees. He designed and also did the physical work himself.

Like all Asuras he wore a crown helmet, dark black with a thin golden border along the rim. The surface of the helmet was uneven and filled with depressions and elevations, with two prominent wooden horn-like structures protruding from two sides asymmetrically. One horn was slightly bigger than the other. Asura Maya bowed to everyone with folded hands.

"It is my pleasure to introduce you everybody here," Krishna wrapped his arms around the man's shoulders and pulled him closer. "Maya, one of the inhabitants of the forests, has personally come to express his thanks to us for saving him from an unexpected man-made disaster."

Yudhishthira got up to greet him. He didn't come closer to Maya because according to the tradition of the Pandavas, once a person sat down for a meal, he couldn't leave the dining area.

"Welcome, welcome...and thank you for coming. It's an honour," Yudhishthira said with a warm smile.

"Thank you, thank you, for saving my family. I am forever indebted to you. I also would like to thank you on behalf of the whole Asura community for granting us land in the new Khandavaprastha," said an emotional Maya.

Krishna patted Maya on the back, trying to make him comfortable.

"I hope that your mission to convert this place into a great city comes true," Maya said with a smile. He was one of the few Asuras who was happy with the Pandava rule in Khandavaprastha and their decision to burn the forests. Maya was happy to have a ruler because he thought this would bring his community more stability and make it more civilised.

"Thank you, it is only because of the encouragement of your people that we are able to move forward. We will always be grateful. And we hope to do you justice," Yudhishthira said.

"And as a token of gratitude, I would like to contribute my architectural skills and help in planning your city," Maya said "I would love to build something unique which will attract people from other areas to visit this new city."

Krishna immediately nodded at Yudhishthira.

"We are delighted by your offer. It's an honour to have a creative genius like you with us. We will have a wonderful time together," Yudhishthira said.

"And now you will have to join us for lunch," Krishna added.

All the Pandavas persuaded Maya to eat with them. He graciously accepted the invitation.

The main problem Khandavaprastha posed for architects according to Vishwakarma was the largely uneven terrain which required intense levelling labour. That was why rebuilding Khandavaprastha was Vishwakarma's most ambitious, difficult and expensive project. The Pandavas had almost invested half of their wealth in Khandavaprastha. They wanted to make this city a marvel and it was a big risk to take on.

Maya's arrival was a godsend. They now had the best team of architects in the country. Together they would rebuild Khandavaprastha and make it a city that would be celebrated for many years to come.

6

Khandavaprastha Gets Ready

The rebuilding of Khandavaprastha was in full flow with a deadline set to finish the outlay of the palace in about a year. Arjuna hardly participated in the rebuilding. He spent a lot of time with his wife. Yudhishthira was the supervisor of the project. Krishna, Vishwakarma and Maya executed his ideas. Bhim always accompanied them. Nakul and Sahadev indulged them whenever they could spare time from their recreational activities.

One night, Arjuna lay on the swing in Draupadi's room. When Draupadi opened the door and walked in, she was shocked to see him there. She shut the door quickly to make sure no one would disturb them.

"What?" Draupadi looked around and continued, "What are you doing here?" Even though she wanted to act like she was worried, her deep blush gave her away. She was very happy to see him.

"You look amazing," Arjuna said, staring at her.

Draupadi was at her stunning best. She had just finished her bath. Her wet hair was slicked back and drops dripped down through her dhoti. She covered her body with her wet towel and a dhoti. Her skin looked smooth and fresh after her bath. Arjuna enjoyed watching her rub lotions on her body. The scent of jasmine aroused him.

She put her hands on his chest and pushed him down on his back. With the support of his chest, she climbed on top of him. He slowly moved his hands and held her waist gently. She kissed him all over his face, but suddenly she looked away, worried.

"What is it?" Arjuna asked, surprised at her behaviour. He sat up, eager to know what was troubling Draupadi.

"You know, Arjuna, I love you more than anyone else but..." She held his face, kissed him a couple of times. "Times are going to change, you know...after the reconstruction of Khandavaprastha, I will have to spend time with your brothers also," she said. "Your brother Yudhishthira is the elder one, and I will have to be with him once he finishes with the reconstruction. We won't be able to spend time like this forever and you know it. This won't last."

Arjuna understood Draupadi. He knew their golden period together would soon come to an end. He knew he loved her more than his brothers, but it didn't matter because in the end she was married to all five Pandavas and each of them had a right to call her their wife. It was a strange situation but the right one. Draupadi had to treat all her husbands equally. That was only fair. She carried the responsibility of providing love and care for the mighty Pandavas and it was no easy task.

"I understand, but that is how it is supposed to be," he consoled her. "We will work something out. Besides, my brothers will take care of you more than me. They will love you more. We have to accept reality and move on. And me, I will always be here," Arjuna whispered.

Draped nodded and kissed him softly on the lips.

"Let us enjoy the time we have now," Arjuna said as he untied her blouse. Draupadi happily let him.

At that moment, the two of them were at the peak of their love. They couldn't let go of each other even for a few seconds. It was the best time of their lives. Arjuna wasn't taking a lot of interest in the reconstruction, so could spend hours with Draupadi. They stayed at the palace and the view was amazing from Draupadi's room. No one bothered them. It was all play and no work for the next couple of years.

7

Indraprastha

After three years of hard work, creativity and determination, the reconstruction was done and the end result was a spectacular display of architectural genius. The Pandavas took a final tour with Krishna and the key architects. A grand ceremony was organised for the inauguration of the new city. Vishwakarma and Maya led the group on the tour, behind them came Yudhishthira with Krishna by his side, then, Bhim, Nakul and Sahadev. Arjuna was last because Draupadi was just behind the group. The two always wanted to stick close to each other. The city was the most well-planned one in the country. The huge investment by the Pandavas had paid off. Vishwakarma had used a lot of new machinery which was developed just for this purpose. The project had been a risky one economically and socially, but the results were stunning.

From the aerial point of view, the city was arranged concentrically. The centre of the city was the Pandavas's palace, the tallest structure in the city. The palace was made from a new fusion metal that had been recently discovered. This was the first structure to be built from the metal. The palace had a broad square base which gradually decreased in size in layers as it towered, the tip being its highest point. This structure would soon be used by architects as the model for all tall buildings because it had beauty, balance and stability.

Around the palace was the first circle with various recreational buildings which included a huge lake. There were a lot of sports facilities, a large lawn, archery galleries and sword fighting arenas. The next circle featured the houses of important ministers, soldiers and major personnel of the court. The third circle was the most innovative and a tourist attraction with many splendid structures. There was a circular building made of copper that was given a wooden finish. The structure had a modest capacity of a hundred people. There was nothing inside it except a few paintings of Lord Shiva, but the special feature was that it was mobile and could be rolled anywhere. The engineering department had designed the rollers which a rider could control just like a chariot. This structure was just a sample. There were hundreds more being built for war purposes and these could be used as movable tents during battle.

Next came the statues of the Pandavas's favourite gods, Shiva and Vishnu. The statues were all depicted in action poses. In one, Lord Shiva was shown leaping with his legs crunched up to his chest and his hands raised above his head. This was a comical pose. In another, Lord Shiva wearing his animal-skin dhoti, was seen standing next to Parvathi, with his arms resting on her shoulder. He was smiling at a serious Parvathi. Yudhishthira had first objected to it, but Krishna's idea had been accepted. In another statue, Vishnu posed dressed in gold armour and with a chakra rotating on his index finger. The chakra glowed yellow. Next to the statues was another major attraction: the dancing fountains.

"This has been done so well, Vishwa. It has turned out to be much better than expected," said Yudhishthira.

"Thank you. But this isn't a solo effort on my part; all of us have dedicated ourselves to make this a beautiful kingdom. I am honoured just to be a part of this project," Vishwakarma said.

Krishna wasn't listening to them. He was busy looking at his own life-sized statue. In it, he held a maroon flute between his lips.

"That is amazing and I really appreciate your token of gratitude but it was totally unnecessary" Krishna said as he admired it.

"You are our guru, guide and teacher. It's only because of you that we could accomplish this. This is just our way of saying thank you," Yudhishthira said.

"Well, thank you then, it's amazing, it does look a lot better than the actual me," Krishna said.

The Pandavas had their statue too. It was situated at the most beautiful junction of Indraprastha so that everybody could see it. Yudhishthira was at the centre, at his side Bhim stood with his golden gada, on another side was Arjuna with his bow arched and aiming at the sky. Nakul and Sahadev were just behind Arjuna. In front of them was their common wife, Draupadi, standing with her hands folded. Vishwakarma also had his statue placed at the beginning of the circle. It was mandatory to have a statue of the person who built the place.

Then came the most illusory and beautiful creation by Asura Maya. This was the Palace of Illusions, a huge, one-storied building. It was made of extensively polished white marble, giving the whole building a shining reflection. The structure was made of a single piece of marble. The whole building looked like a huge square. The entrance had huge, thick, supporting pillars. There were various levels cut at respective heights. At the topmost point, centrally, was a huge pearl. It was an oval, sea-blue pearl, and the sunlight reflecting off it gave it the appearance of a water-filled gem, a giant bubble of water.

Every corner of the interior looked like magic. There were not a lot of rooms and courts in the palace. It was just one floor but it had a huge surface area. The architectural specialty of the hall was that there were just two pillars on either side to support the structure. The floor was well-polished marble, shining and reflecting the ceiling. The ceiling itself was also made of marble, with wonderful designs of ancient stick diagrams portraying the origin of the human species. So, the whole floor would appear to be patterned with images because of the reflections. Asura Maya had told Krishna that he would keep changing the images every year to maintain variety. The Pandavas were just roaming around the hall, enjoying the structures. The bright lighting was a key feature that they liked. The lights were not situated in the ceiling. They were on the pillars on either side, at the corners and the hinges of the flooring and also on the ceiling, thus giving the floor additional illumination.

As Bhim walked across the hall, he accidentally stepped on water which rose up to his knees.

"Oh, yes, that is a real catch; it is a pond I have made to blend in with the room. It is considered to be good luck. So, I decided to go with it," Asura Maya said.

The Pandavas mocked Bhim for his lack of awareness. No one else had noticed it either. It was just that Bhim was ahead of them and so he had fallen for the trap. Little did he know that this pond would be known in the history books as one of the main factors for the Kurukshetra war.

"Since, the water is crystal clear, it reflects the images from the ceiling and thus it becomes difficult to notice the water. Water in the hall brings good luck," Asura Maya added.

"Beautiful, Maya," Krishna patted Maya on his back.

"Maya, you know we are blessed to have a talent like you with us. This is the best thing I have seen so far. We are all proud of you," Yudhishthira said.

Arjuna also applauded him. He knew nothing about this. He was the smallest contributor to all of this. Even Nakul and Sahadev had helped a lot during these years. Arjuna was ashamed of himself. He hadn't helped his brothers when it was most needed but he was relieved that they had done such a good job. His brothers had never questioned him for not participating in the construction.

"The city is great but have you peopled decided on a name for it? Since it's been rebuilt it's only logical to rename it," Krishna suggested.

He was right, Khandavaprastha meant wasteland and it didn't quite fit the new city.

"Yes, we need to rename it. New city, new name," Bhim agreed. He was more involved with the physical aspects of things and rarely participated in suggesting original ideas. Either he agreed with them or he didn't.

"Okay, we need to think of something fast, our ceremony is tomorrow and we don't even have a name. A city has to have a name." Yudhishthira was starting to panic.

Everybody went quiet, thinking of a perfect name.

"I have a very interesting and fitting name in mind," Krishna said. It was like the city had instantly responded by bestowing the name on him. He always came up with the best names and solutions. "Indraprastha, the land of Lord Indra. This is what it is. We have built the most beautiful city on earth just like Lord Indra's country up in the skies. This is a suitable name for us."

Yudhishthira thought about it. Indraprastha was a very good name. It was easy to pronounce and easy to remember. He didn't have any other names and there was no time to waste.

"I like it. Let's go with Indraprastha. Anybody with better suggestions?" he asked and waited for five seconds before it was decided.

No objections, everybody liked it. The land of Lord Indra.

"Indraprastha is the name," Yudhishthira declared.

After naming the city, they had a few more things left to discuss about the next day. So, they stayed up all night talking.

8

The Conflict over Draupadi

The Inauguration at which Indraprastha was declared the capital of the Pandavas was a spectacular extravaganza. The concentric city and every layer of it were decorated with different kinds of lights. Every building, structure and statue was well polished and a guide was posted next to each one to describe it. The princes, kings and tourism experts from all over the country were invited. Even Dhritarashtra and the Kauravas came just to show the public they were supportive. The Kauravas were looking at the unexpected. The organisation and the creativity on display immediately earned a lot of interest from the kings. Some of them even gave contracts to the Pandavas and Vishwakarma to build their cities. The Pandavas profited more than double the amount they had invested in the city in the first week itself through tourists and commercial investments. Greater the risks, greater the rewards!

Over the next year, the influence, status and fame of the Pandavas kept increasing. They had become the most sought after builders in the country. They had received numerous contracts and their fortune was now much bigger than that of the Kauravas and the whole of Hastinapur.

Yudhishthira had started getting recognition for his work and was a more relaxed person now. He assigned most of the work to his assistants. He had started to spend some time with his wife. Yudhishthira was constantly taking Draupadi to ceremonies and meetings and involving her in his work more.

Even Bhim started spending time with her. He took her with him to watch his training sessions and also trained her a little. Draupadi enjoyed their company. Nakul and Sahadev had grown to become the most handsome men in the country. They separately charmed their wife. Their sessions with her were mostly spent talking and understanding each other. They admired Draupadi's beauty and showered her with gifts. The brothers took really good care of her.

Arjuna's time with his wife had been cut down. Krishna and he dedicated a lot of time to discussing philosophy and the necessity of training. Arjuna was training for a big battle with the Kauravas.

* * *

Draupadi and Arjuna were standing next to the highest water fountain in Indraprastha and in the entire country. It was a unique tribute to the previous inhabitants of the land–the Nagas and the Asuras. There was a five-headed cobra at the centre with its mouth open, and water shot out from the mouths horizontally. The height of the snake was almost the same as that of the Palace of Illusions. Surrounding the Naga were the statues of a typical Asura on guard, water flowing from his horns upwards, to a great height.

"This is the most beautiful city your brothers have created," Draupadi said.

Arjuna didn't reply. He felt as if she was taunting him with the statement. She knew he hadn't worked with the city's re-modelling. He wanted to remind her that he had left his brothers so that he could spend time with her. But he controlled himself.

"Yudhishthira, Bhim, Nakul, Sahadev and you have invested so much and made this into a success," she continued.

Now she was hurting Arjuna, but he knew he deserved it. He kept quiet.

"You know, I still remember that night you came to my room," Draupadi continued. "You told me that your brothers would take good care of me. And you are right. I am actually enjoying their company now. Last night I spoke to Nakul and I was surprised. He gave me a lot of jewelry and then we spoke about the reasons we like each other. He has become a handsome man."

Draupadi showed him the gold bracelets and necklaces he had given her. They looked good on her.

"Yes, I remember," Arjuna replied and looked away. He wasn't afraid to show his discontentment. He was sure that his relationship with Draupadi was on the decline. Their bond wasn't special anymore.

"Look, Arjuna," she said. "I know all of this is bothering you and I felt that way too. It took me time but now I am really happy with all of you. I am happy with my life. Your brothers are good people, they are also my husbands. I need to spend some time with them. It's only fair."

"Yes, they are my brothers and have every right over you as much as me," Arjuna who was looking at the water, now, turned to face Draupadi.

Draupadi tried to speak but Arjuna continued before she opened her mouth. He wanted to tell what he was feeling.

"You know I don't have the same feelings I had for you before. You don't really seem to care about me anymore. Yes, my brothers are great but what about me? Does this mean we can't have the relationship we shared before? Does that mean I'm not special anymore? I was the one who fought for you at the swayamvar, the only man to lift the bow and hit the eye. I am the one who won you at the swayamvar..."

"No, Arjuna, it's not like that. I still love you, and I still want to relive those moments we shared in the past years, but you know, things aren't the same. You have to understand I have a responsibility. I can't just be with you the whole time," Draupadi pleaded.

This was a devastating blow to Arjuna. He had got his answer, she wasn't only his anymore. That time had passed. The pain was unbearable but he managed to fake a laugh.

"I always thought that this... us... the time we spent with each other, that would be forever... but now I know, and I appreciate you telling me how you feel. It really solves everything. I don't have to keep thinking about you now; I don't have to worry about you. Now there are a lot of people to care about you. It's fine. It's just that I didn't see it because I was blindly in love with you," he said.

Draupadi remained silent. He was being a bit too extreme, but he was right.

Arjuna sighed heavily and continued, "I don't know about you but I can't keep things this way. I love you too much to watch you with others even if they are my own brothers. I will find a solution. I will discuss this with Krishna and my brothers tomorrow."

Draupadi's eyes were filled with tears. She hadn't expected Arjuna to be this aggressive.

Arjuna saw her crying and it hurt him to see her like this. "I'm sorry about this, but a decision needs to be taken," he said as he walked off.

Draupadi stood by herself on the balcony, the moonlight falling on her. She cried for a long time before she went back to one of her husbands.

9

Narad Muni's Solution

The brothers called Narad Muni to decide about Draupadi. Narad Muni was the most efficient problem-solver and the Pandavas always consulted him on thorny issues. The Pandavas, Krishna and Narad gathered in the hall. Draupadi stood at the opposite end of the hall. None of them were seated. The atmosphere was more tense and nervous than it was when they had discussed war and tactics against the Kauravas.

Narad Muni was the calmest among them, and the main reason why he was able to take important decisions in stressful conditions was this quality. Narad Muni trained most of his pupils also to be calm during difficult times. He had acquired this quality after years of meditation. His pupils went on to become great leaders and captains of well-known sports teams thanks to him.

Narad Muni had not cut his hair and as a result, his rough hair had grown till his shoulders. He had a small bun on top of his head and let the rest of his hair loose. This look would later be emulated by most youngsters in Indraprastha. Narad Muni was a moderately-built man and well nourished. He wore a broad, bright orange angavastram over his abdomen accompanied by a matching dhoti. He always looked very comfortable in his attire. Narad Muni was famous for his musical skills. He played the veena every day and since he was such a musical person he needed to carry around something to keep the beat. So, he had two wooden flaps attached to his wrist, and on bringing his fingers closer to his palm, the two flaps would create a beat at his touch.

Narad Muni wanted his guru, Krishna's, blessings. Krishna was delighted to see him after a long time and gave him a tight hug. Narad Muni and Krishna has solved many a crisis together. Both were masterminds. Both could conquer the world effortlessly.

"Greetings, everyone," Narad Muni said. "How are you, Pandavas? It's been a long time since we met. Bhim, you seem to have grown quite a lot, working out a lot. Nakul, Sahadev, what handsome men you have become! Arjuna, wonderful to see you. Yudhishthira, wonderful job with the city," he said as he greeted each of them.

"Greetings, Queen Draupadi," he said, turning to her.

She gave him a weak, forced smile. The only reason she smiled back was because he was her elder and she respected him.

Narad Muni could feel the tension ramping up in the room. And he sensed it was all about Draupadi. He knew that with matters of the heart, nothing was easy.

Yudhishthira wanted to find a solution and immediately opened his case, "Narad Muni, as you know, our marriage is a bit different and unique and so we are experiencing some major problems. We five brothers are sharing our wife, Draupadi. The problem is that we all love her and want to spend time with her. We are lost about dividing her among ourselves equally. So, it is only fair that I ask you to decide and tell us how to proceed."

Narad Muni nodded. Polyandry was common but all the husbands being brothers wasn't common, especially if the brothers were celebrities like the Pandavas and always in the public eye. This was the rarest of rare cases.

"We can't just divide her time equally among us. There is some part of her which each of us will miss if we do that. We need to have her with us like any other normal wife. This part-time wife scenario will be the death of our relationship," Nakul said, showing that even he was extremely unhappy. It was rare for Nakul to be unhappy with anything. It showed how big a problem sharing Draupadi was.

"Yes, now, we don't get proper time to spend with her. She is constantly moving around and it disturbs us a lot. Narad Muni, it just doesn't feel right. That's not how a husband and wife relationship should be," Sahadev added.

"Narad Muni, please find a solution. I don't want to see us brothers fighting each other over it," Bhim said.

Arjuna didn't speak. He was feeling bad for Draupadi. It was because of him that all of the other brothers were indirectly blaming her for their dissatisfaction.

"Arjuna, do you have something to say?" Narad Muni asked. He wanted to know what everybody felt about this before he took a decision.

"Yes, we need you to find a solution for this. That seems to be the only logical thing to do," Arjuna said in a pained tone.

Draupadi was crushed to hear these words from Arjuna again.

"Okay, there is only one clear solution. This is how it will be," Narad Muni moved closer to the Pandavas. "Since all of you love her equally, all of you deserve equal time and privacy," he said. "So, Draupadi will rotate among you. She will spend one full year with one brother alone, during that one year; she will have no communication with the others except during court meeting or other gatherings. Then, the next year, she will move on to the next brother, and every year after she finishes with one brother, she will drink the special liquid which I will provide her. This will make her body pure again, giving all the brothers the same Draupadi each time. And it is a fair proposition. Privacy is an important factor in this arrangement. So, if any of the other brothers try to interfere or even by mistake enter the space Draupadi and her husband are in, that person will be exiled from Indraprastha. This may seem a little extreme but it is the only way to maintain discipline and respect among the brothers. It will be helpful in the long term for all."

The Pandavas processed the plan for a few minutes. All of them liked the solution.

"But who is going first, who is second? What is the order, Narad Muni?" Arjuna asked nervously.

"Yes, that is simple to solve. Let's go according to tradition here. The eldest one is first, then the second eldest and so on. Since Yudhishthira is the eldest, he will rightfully be the first one to have Draupadi in his first year, and then comes Bhim, then you, then Nakul and Sahadev. Any problems with that?" Narad Muni looked around.

No problems. Even if they had some, no one opposed him.

Arjuna was third on the list. This gave him a two-year term before he could have Draupadi as his wife. The next couple of months were very depressing for him. He would just stay in his room and most of the time, he just ate and slept. He gained a lot of weight during that period. He didn't participate in training, didn't do administrative work and didn't talk to anyone. He was doing nothing at all. He desperately needed motivation and consolation to get over Draupadi's absence.

* * *

Arjuna and Krishna were sitting in the palace gardens one day. Arjuna had been there for hours. That was Arjuna's daily routine now; eating, sitting in the garden doing nothing. He had lost interest in life itself. The garden was the perfect place to relax. It was Arjuna's daily dose of medication, his place of solitude and comfort.

Krishna sat next to him in silence for a few minutes, looking at the beautiful yellow tulips. The petals were large and symmetrical. It was rare to see such a perfect flower.

Finally, Krishna broke the silence. "How are you?" he asked. "It's been some time since we spoke. You don't step out very often."

"Yes, I stay in my room, reading. It helps me." Arjuna read history, concentrating on battles and trade deals.

"Listen, Arjuna, I know you are going through a difficult time with all that's going on with Draupadi," Krishna said in a soothing tone. "I know how it's to not see the woman you love, not to be with her, but you can't do this to yourself. You look miserable. You can't let life beat you. It's difficult but what isn't? You have to stay strong and focus on the future. You still have a long life to live. Make yourself useful. Make a mark on this world like you are meant to. Stop feeling sorry for yourself."

He leaned forward as he continued, "Life is hard, and this is the hardest part of it all. To stay away from the ones you love the most is a challenge. But, you have to continue living, you just cannot waste your time thinking about the past. And you, being the king, have great power and a responsibility to change the world. So, start doing it." Krishna also had not seen Radha for almost a year, since the reconstruction of Indraprastha. He missed her a lot but he carried on with the hope that he would meet her again soon.

Krishna's words brought Arjuna to his senses. He had the power to change the world and he couldn't let it go to waste. He was in terrible shape. He had gained a lot of weight and his strong chest had become soft and saggy. His beard was unkempt and his hair was a mess. He felt disgusted at himself. This was the turning point.

Krishna always said, "Always look at yourself in the mirror, always introspect."

An inspired Arjuna started training the next day.

10

Arjuna in Training

He started his training the very next day. He wanted to get back in shape and reach his previous standard of fitness. So, he asked Krishna to be his personal trainer. They worked out seven days a week, thrice a day. Morning sessions included running up the hills and climbing many flights of stairs. Afternoon sessions were weight training, where he would go to the forest and lift heavy logs of wood. He mostly concentrated on his arms, legs and the core muscles as they played a major role in archery. The evening sessions involved ground exercise.

Slowly, Arjuna resumed his archery training as well. Krishna suggested subtle improvements on how to aim and release the bow which Arjuna mastered quickly. Next came target practice with wooden targets. This was also easy but it took him longer than he had anticipated. This was followed by the moving targets, then, close hand-to-hand combat, and the secondary usage of the arrow for combat where he used it as a knife. There were also sword fights which he didn't like very much. He wanted to reach the highest level in archery so that there would be no situation where he would have to use a sword.

In six months, he was better and stronger than ever. He was in the best shape of his life. He grew a thick moustache curling upwards at the ends, and also kept some light stubble. He wore some accessories too. He liked wearing diamond-studded, square earrings on his right ear. He wore a thin bracelet on his left arm right on his biceps. His torturous fitness routine and training were now the talk of Indraprastha. The girls in the city swooned all over him and he enjoyed the attention. Arjuna realised he was a free man for the next couple of years while Draupadi was with his brothers. He wasn't bound by the rules of marriage or tied to one person during that time.

Draupadi could only cry when she saw Arjuna with other women, but she made it a point to let Arjuna know about it. She sent messages through her faithful maids to Arjuna, but there was no response. She even went to the extent of trying to convince him of secretly meeting her. Nothing worked. Arjuna had headed in a new direction now.

Arjuna began advanced training. On a fateful day, he was standing alone inside a circle in the middle of the training ground with his bow and a handful of arrows, his legs tied to the ground with chains. He couldn't run, only adjust his legs a little. At a radius of 20 metres were war horses with modified targets. The targets were metal-sculpted warriors. Arjuna was ready. If he hit the targets, it would halt the horse in its tracks. There was no guarantee that the horse would stop but this was high-level training and it was a challenge he had to meet. Arjuna had to hit the targets from a certain set distance. Arjuna loaded his first arrow, pulled it halfway and pointed it at the floor. He then closed his eyes to concentrate on his muscles, his mind. The light flowing down from the top focused on him. He was centre stage.

All the other warriors stopped their training sessions to witness Arjuna's performance.

Krishna signalled at the horse keepers. They let the horses run free. All at once, from all sides, the horses galloped towards Arjuna at full speed. These horses were trained war stallions. The best in the country. For a few milliseconds Arjuna just stood still, analysing the horses's pattern, then, he started releasing his arrows in quick succession. All his arrows were headshots, but he had to keep turning to cover the circumference.

It was an amazing display of archery skills. Arjuna was better than before, sharper, more accurate and more focused with no Draupadi to distract him. From the top viewing gallery, Arjuna looked like a rotating machine, spraying arrows in all directions and the horses kept slowing down in their tracks as the targets fell.

Krishna observed his disciple from a distance. Arjuna looked like the warrior hero he was destined to be. His hair had grown long now, some of the locks touching his forehead. The rest of his hair was flowing in the breeze. His pupils were constricted and focused for long-range targets, not one horse had even travelled half the distance of the radius. His chest was continuously getting pumped by the quick releases of the arrows. On loading an arrow, his chest pumped up, his biceps and forearms tightened and on release, the muscles relaxed. This required tremendous stamina which he had gained by daily long-distance runs and mountain climbing.

Almost all the horses had been hit. There were just three left, but when Arjuna reached for his arrow he realised that it was his last one. He had to hit three with one. And the three horses were aligned next to each other, not one after the other.

It all came down to Krishna's words. He had once told Arjuna, "Always be the smarter man. Be patient, calm and ruthless."

Arjuna stood in position. He didn't aim for the head this time. He hit one horse, initiating a spinning motion with his arm, which knocked off the other two with its momentum. The horses stopped right before him. Everyone applauded Arjuna's feat. The women around him went crazy. "Please marry me," "I love you," they shouted.

Arjuna raised his hands to acknowledge the applause. He had become the hero he was always meant to be... Krishna was delighted at his pupil's success. When an elated Arjuna returned to the palace, he was congratulated by Bhim. News of his feat had reached the palace very fast. The palace guards had a difficult time keeping Arjuna's fan from entering the building. The crowd was massive. It didn't matter what he did, however big or small his victory, the masses loved him. His aura was something other people could only dream of. Arjuna walked past a long line of place officials and went to his room. Finally, he could rest in peace, eat his favourite cashew nuts, enjoy a sweet and salty lemon drink and relax on his comfortable bed.

11

The Unfortunate Incident

Just as Arjuna fell asleep, his personal guard, Ranga, knocked on his door. Arjuna woke up.

"Master, there is a peasant who is desperately asking for you," Ranga said.

"Why, what's the matter?" Arjuna sat up in bed.

"It seems he has been robbed of his cattle by an intruder from the outskirts of the forest. He has been crying and begging to meet you. He says that the cattle were the only way to sustain his livelihood. He is desperate for help."

Arjuna mulled over the problem as he ate a couple of cashew nuts.

"Master, should I give him the money for the cattle and send him back?" Ranga suggested. He didn't want such a small thing to disturb the great warrior. Arjuna left his room before Ranga could say more. It was evening and he was almost certain that Draupadi and Yudhishthitra were together in their room. According to the rules of Narad Muni, one brother couldn't enter the room when the other was busy with the wife. It would lead to exile. A simple rule to follow or break.

Arjuna knew it but he kept going. After his training, he had met Yudhishthira and received some praise from his elder brother. He had also seen him go to his room. The trouble was Arjuna had no string left in his bow, he needed a new one and Yudhishthira had stored all the backup weapons in a secure place next to his room. But to enter that secure place, he needed to pass through his brother's room.

"It doesn't matter, he might be alone now," Arjuna told Ranga as they walked down the corridor.

"Master, let me take a look and tell you," Ranga tried.

"It's already too late for the cattle rearer; it's a question of his livelihood. I have to go help him."

Yudhishthira's room was at the opposite wing of the same floor and there were a flight of steps leading to it. Arjuna walked quickly and reached the door. Ranga caught up. Arjuna flung it open and walked straight to the weaponry. He didn't look at his brother's bed which was next to him. This was it. Arjuna had entered the room on purpose when Yudhishthira and Draupadi were alone. He had broken the pact. Yudhishthira and Draupadi were in bed together. They were so shocked that they couldn't react. Ranga witnessed this from the outside. He couldn't imagine the consequences of all this. It had happened too fast for him to react.

Arjuna picked up what he needed and went on to complete his task. He retrieved the animals for the cattle rearer. It turned out to be a petty issue in the end. One of the Asuras had captured the cattle and was taking them to the forest. Arjuna tracked down the Asura and got them back. It was an easy task which could have been performed by any of his soldiers. He did what he thought was right at the moment, but looking back, even he knew that the poor man wasn't worth the consequences he was going to face. Or maybe he wanted to get away from the palace and the city in his heart of hearts.

It was very early and the sun hadn't even risen. Only the Pandavas, Krishna, Draupadi and Ranga were in the palace hall. All of them were tearful except Arjuna and Krishna (no one had ever seen him crying). Arjuna packed all his stuff, wrapped them in a cloth and placed them near his feet. There was no sadness or guilt on his face. He was taking his exile very well.

"Arjuna, please try and understand the situation, it's not your fault that you entered our room for the wellbeing of a citizen," Yudhishthira said. "It was your duty. Please listen to us. The pact can be changed. You don't have to go."

Yudhishthira walked closer to Arjuna and held his shoulders with a firm grip. He wanted to remind Arjuna how much they loved him and how this decision would impact Indraprastha. The departure of any of the Pandavas would make the people speculate about problems among the brothers. It would make them lose confidence in the Pandavas. Many would question their unity.

Arjuna looked at his brother's red eyes and smiled as if he had already known about this. "Yes, brother, I realise it," he said. "But I must follow protocol. I have broken the pact no matter what the reason. There were a lot of ways in which I could have solved this. None is immune from a holy pact, a prince or a peasant. Don't worry about me. Indraprastha will be a better place when I return." Arjuna put his arm on his brother's, trying to comfort him.

Arjuna's exile was deemed more of a choice rather than a consequence of a pact. He was never fond of rules. A solitary time was what he wanted. Yudhishthira didn't reply. He knew that no matter how much he or his brothers tried, Arjuna would only do what he wanted. Krishna didn't participate in this, he was just listening. Maybe even he wanted Arjuna to experience the world and learn something. Krishna wanted to make Arjuna the best and to be the best; he had to face uncomfortable situations. Arjuna had to take strong decisions and risks. Bhim knew Arjuna too well to convince him to stay. Arjuna had already decided to leave. He gave Arjuna a hug.

"See you soon, Bhim. Keep up the training. We'll meet again," Arjuna said fondly.

Bhim loved Arjuna, and he hugged him tightly.

Arjuna went to Nakul and Sahadev and hugged both of them. They were his favourites and he took care of them as if they were his children. He had taught them everything he knew and hoped they would become great men. He was very proud of them.

"I will be back soon. Take care of yourselves," he bid them goodbye.

Then he walked to his master, Krishna, and touched his feet. Krishna looked into his eyes. He expected his favourite pupil to learn something from his exile. Arjuna then walked to Yudhishthira and touched his feet.

Yudhishthira blessed him, "Take care of yourself out there."

Arjuna had very little luggage. He had his bow on his back, all his clothes tied up and bundled together and slung on his shoulders. Nothing else. He passed by Draupadi as he walked away. He knew she was in pain even if she wasn't crying. He didn't console her. He left without saying goodbye.

ULUPI

12

Arjuna Meets Ulupi

Arjuna wanted a solitary life. He wanted to experience this self-imposed pilgrimage to the fullest. But the poor Brahmin whose cattle he had retrieved convinced him to take his son with him as his protector. Arjuna didn't need any guard but he finally agreed, saying that the son would accompany him only till the point he chose. Solitude was a great teacher for Arjuna. He relied on being alone during difficult times. Moments to reflect reveal the truth of existence; we live alone and die alone. A solitary journey would have a profound impact on him.

Arjuna and his guard walked every day and set up temporary shelters from leaves and small wooden sticks. The Brahmin helped him with his learning. Arjuna slowly and steadily became comfortable with the nomadic forest life. They would first travel for a few days in daylight and rest at night under the trees once they found a good spot by a water body. Arjuna ate whatever was available, a hunted deer would last for a couple days but he mostly stuck to fruits.

Arjuna had some arrows, but he also made a few from wood. For carrying water, he used snake skin. He had pulled the outer skin of the reptile cleanly and tied both ends together. Conveniently, he tied it around his waist.

His appearance also had changed. His moustache was no longer curled upwards. His hair which was already long and wavy had become extremely thick. He didn't use the expensive creams and herbals he used back in Indraprastha. He only washed himself in water. But he managed to keep himself clean and free from major diseases although a bout of diarrhoea did trouble him for a few weeks.

* * *

He had chosen his spot perfectly at the starting point of the river in the north of the country where the forest wasn't very thick and dense. There was no threat from wild animals, only a few small animals like birds, deer and a snake or two which Arjuna knew how to handle well. Arjuna and the Brahmin boy first made their hut, which was built to last longer this time. The hut was just like the one Arjuna and the Pandavas built when they were in hiding after the house of wax incident. The Brahmin boy was a budding chemist and he made a paste to bind the building together.

The ceiling of the hut was a well-carved sheet of wood, which gave them shelter. The floor was levelled with matted and dry leaves. Arjuna had his routine. He woke up at sunrise and went to the water body which was just 500 metres away. The sound of the river could be heard from their hut. He would go for a swim and then explore the forest for food. The boy sometimes accompanied or he would stay back in the hut, reading and cooking.

One day, Arjuna went deeper into the forest. He heard the sound of splashing water. Suddenly, Arjuna was on alert.

A person in the forest is there for two reasons: either he is on exile from his native land or he lives there. Both could be dangerous. So, Arjuna hid behind a tree and spotted a few girls bathing.

Some of them were half-covered but fully wet, some didn't have anything on but they were neck deep in water. Two of them were floating, giggling, playing with each other, and splashing water on a girl who had just stepped in. She was wearing a single dhoti and a white piece of cloth across her shoulders which was now wet. Another girl was peacefully floating. She caught his eye and the sun's rays. Her skin glistened as she stepped out.

The other girls stepped out too and started drying themselves on land. They helped each other get dressed. Ulupi, the girl who held Arjuna under her spell, had perfect features, with arched eyebrows and a chiselled jaw. She wore a small nose ring and an arm band which had the image of a Naga in the centre of it. The other girls had finished, they were all almost dressed. They all wore the same tiny, white blouses and short dhotis. Arjuna wondered how dangerous it was for such a beautiful group of women to be all by themselves in the forest.

It looked like Ulupi, the girl of his dreams, would stay there for a bit longer. She told the others to leave and sat by the river. It was time for her to change into her dry clothes. She looked perfect to Arjuna. He was so engrossed in her that he stumbled and stood in open view. He couldn't just run away, it would be insulting on his part. The best option was to apologise.

"I'm sorry; I didn't mean to jump out like this. I mean, I wasn't hiding out there or stalking you or anything...I was just passing by," he said, running out of words soon.

Ulupi raised her eyebrows, demanding more of an explanation. That wasn't enough for her.

"I was just passing by, I'm sorry." He took a few steps back. Running away seemed to be a viable option.

"Don't worry about it, it happens right." Ulupi said, surprisingly. Maybe she was used to such things.

Arjuna nodded, relieved. She seemed to be at ease about the whole situation.

Ulupi walked away from the water and closer to the trees where Arjuna was standing. "I know you are surprised to find me along the banks of a river on the middle of the forest, so, let me introduce myself. I am Ulupi, the Naga Princess of the Airavata clan and daughter of King Kauravaya, the leader of the Airavat clan. My palace is along the banks of the River Ganga. My friends and I love to swim in this river," she smiled.

Arjuna couldn't believe that he was looking at a Naga Princess, moreover, he had seen her naked. It was a crime in most of the kingdoms. Even though he didn't have any personal grudges with the Nagas, the Pandavas as a whole were not on talking terms with the Nagas. So, he didn't know how she would react to his introduction.

"Pleasure to meet you Princess," he said, bowing in respect. "I am Arjuna, one of the Pandavas, the rulers of Indraprastha."

"Actually, to be honest, I have noticed you a few times in the past month. You live near the river?" the Princess asked. "What is a prince, a ruler of the most wanted kingdom on land doing in the middle of the forest? Are you staying in the forest for any specific reason?"

"Yes. I am on a pilgrimage here for a year. I left Indraprastha. Now, I am on a journey to explore and learn. To enjoy our lovely planet."

"So, are you enjoying your time near the River Ganges? Good. Even I love the Ganges; it's an amazing and refreshing sight."

"Yes, I love the forest and the Ganges. It's been a thrilling journey till now."

"Come, let me walk you back to your hut," she said.

"No, I will go by myself. I think you are getting late. I'm sorry about the hindrance caused by me."

"Let me walk with you. It is a privilege to have met a great warrior like you. Let me accompany you," she requested.

Arjuna couldn't be rude to such a beautiful woman. "Of course, it's an honour. I don't meet a Naga Princess every day," he said.

Ulupi walked with Arjuna to his hut. Arjuna didn't want her to get too close to him, but he also couldn't tell her to leave. She was a Naga and he didn't want to say anything to upset her.

When they got close to the hut, Arjuna spotted the boy stocking up wood for the fire.

"Okay ..." Arjuna bid a hasty farewell to Ulupi. "Thanks for walking me back." Arjuna wanted to wrap this up as soon as possible. He didn't want the boy to see them talking.

"I loved your company, so, maybe we can meet tomorrow also. I will show you my palace by the side of the river. I know you will adore it," Ulupi said.

Arjuna tackled the invite right away. "It would be nice, but I am planning continue my journey tomorrow," he said. "I will be moving farther into the course of river. I have plans to travel the whole of the north of the country including the north eastern parts and so, I have to keep moving quickly."

"Well, that's not a problem. You can leave a few days later. You have the whole year and I know the routes in the forest inside out. I will tell you about the routes that will lead you to your destination faster. I insist you come with me tomorrow, you will enjoy it, I am sure," Ulupi said.

Arjuna could see that she wouldn't let him go that easily. What was the worst that could happen? He decided to spend a day with her, then say goodbye forever.

"Yes, I will be here tomorrow," he said.

Arjuna went back to his hut. He watched the Brahmin boy who had come along with him. The reason Arjuna had brought the boy along was to teach him archery and some philosophy. He wanted to show him how to survive in the wild, but he wasn't comfortable watching the boy do all the hard work while he was busy enjoying life with a beautiful Naga Princess. It was not ethical. So, he decided to send the boy back home.

The boy left early the next day, carrying the food supplies that were required for his journey back. Now it was just Arjuna and Ulupi.

13

The Naga-Hunter Conflict

The next day, when Arjuna went for his morning swim, Ulupi was waiting for him. He found it strange that she knew the timings of his daily activities. A little too enthusiastic for their second meet!

"Glad to see you again and thanks for staying back. It will be worth the wait, you will see," she said with a smile, genuinely happy to see him.

Arjuna smiled at her. He looked beautiful and he felt very attracted to her.

"Okay, let's start out," she said, eager to show him her home. "My palace is next to the river on the other bank. It will take us a couple of hours to get there."

Just about half an hour into the walk, they heard the rumbling of bushes and the sound of people running and shouting.

"Take cover," Ulupi instructed Arjuna as she camouflaged herself in the branches. Arjuna was new here and didn't know what was happening, so he followed orders. He hid behind Ulupi.

They silently waited. Arjuna never took cover behind anyone but the smartest warriors are the ones who survive by any means, even if it is by hiding behind some one. Arjuna couldn't help but notice Ulupi's bare back. Ulupi was crouching, her back arched, her skin moist from sweat droplets due to the heat. Her skin was golden, her waist, shapely. Arjuna couldn't take his eyes off her.

"I think we are in the clear now," Ulupi said.

The sounds gradually faded in the background.

"What was that?" he asked, guessing it was a pack of animals passing by.

"They are the hunters," Ulupi said. "We have been fighting them for some time now but they always come back for the Nagas. They hunt snakes for the skin."

Ulupi turned around to face Arjuna. She stood very close to him. He could feel her breath on his face. It was intense and he felt uncomfortable.

"They are greedy, ruthless and hungry for money," she explained. "They would kill just about anything to make money. And also, they are exceptionally well-trained and strong, born hunters, their ancestors were the greatest hunters on land and they try to honour that legacy. But now they are just savages killing for fun. They have been hunting our species for many years and we try to stop them. It's been a tough fight for us."

"How many are they?" he asked as he stood up.

"Not many, just five. But highly skilled," she said.

"Maybe this time, you can drive them away forever with my help," Arjuna said.

"Yes, maybe, but we need to know more about them before we attack." Ulupi shared the entire history of the hunters with Arjuna. Their history was long and over a hundred years old. Their ancestors, the first hunters, had mostly hunted just for food and survival but as the generations passed, greed grew. They started hunting elephants for ivory, animals for skin. The market for snake skin was new and untapped.

Arjuna was all set to attack them. He persuaded Ulupi to take him to their base. The base comprised of three tents. Piles of wood were stacked outside them. A young man was sitting on a rock sharpening a knife. Another was assessing the day's collection. These hunters made their living by selling animal skin and parts to the palaces. They had a wide range including elephant tusks, tiger skin and snake skin. The environmentalists of the Airavat clan had been battling the poachers for decades in vain.

Arjuna and Ulupi scanned the setting carefully. The plan was simple, to attack when the hunters least expected it. The bigger hunter called out to the younger one for help to arrange the elephant tusks. The younger hunter immediately went across to help. They had collected a lot of elephant tusks. The bigger, whiter, more valuable tusks went into one bag and the smaller ones into a different one. The big tusks were sold to kings who would display them in their palaces. Arjuna remembered that there were many items of furniture made of ivory in Hastinapur. He was repulsed by them. He would make sure Indraprastha did no harm to elephants.

Three more hunters entered; the biggest of them (who was much smaller than Arjuna) was carrying a dead deer with an arrow embedded in it. He had a big smile on his lips. It was a good day for them. The other hunters held bows, arrows and knives. They wore animal skins–tiger, deer and half-tiger, half-leopard ones. They didn't wear dhotis. Animal skins were wrapped around their waists as well.

The man who seemed like the leader sat abruptly and exhaled deeply. Their day's work was over. They could eat happily and rest now.

"Good day, boys, it's been a very good day," he said.

The others agreed with him and patted each other's backs.

"But unfortunately, couldn't find any of those bloody snakes," he said, frustrated. Orders from all over the country had made him desperate for more snake skin.

"We have to try again tomorrow, and we need to make sure we get a lot of them," the biggest man said.

"Those bloody Nagas and the Airavat clan aren't making life easier for us. We need to get rid of them if we want to do this. Once we finish off selling our last batch of the season, we have to take care of the Airavat clan permanently. It will certainly help our sales for the next season," the leader suggested.

All of them agreed and proceeded to eat their tender cooked meat. They focused completely on the food and stopped listening to their leader.

Arjuna and Ulupi who had been observing the group for the last hour sensed an opportunity.

"Now is the time, they are too involved in their food, we need to go now," Arjuna whispered.

Ulupi nodded.

His sling arrows would immobilise his targets by encircling them. Arjuna crawled to a perfect spot. Precision and speed were crucial in this mission. He loaded his first sling. He would aim at their torsos since they were seated. He had to hit their shoulders or feet to paralyse them. First, he hit the biggest man and he was on target. The rope wound itself around the shoulders of the man who was munching on a hunk of meat. He fell to the ground with his arms pinned to his sides. The others were alerted to the danger, but there was little they could do. Arjuna felled the rest and Ulupi delivered a deadly blow to the head to one of them. The young boy remained, trapped and scared.

"Son, the group you were a part of was the wrong one. You have made a mistake but it can be rectified," Arjuna said, not too harshly. "Animals have as much a right to live as us. Find another way to make a living. Respect Mother Nature and you will be happy."

The captured poachers were transported to the Airavat prison. Arjuna and Ulupi gave the young boy a second chance at life.

14

Ulupi's Proposal

"I am forever indebted to you for your service to the Airavat clan. It means a lot to us," Ulupi said.

"It's my duty to protect Mother Nature and besides, they needed to be stopped. What they were doing was pure evil and evil has to be defeated. Thank you for letting me know about this problem. Hunting and poaching animals has been on the rise. Poaching is an issue all kingdoms need to address for the wellbeing of society," Arjuna said with a smile.

Arjuna expected her to speak but she didn't. Neither of them said anything for a few seconds.

"Ok, it's getting dark. It's getting late for you too. I better head back to my hut," he said. He didn't like to walk at night and he needed at least a couple of hours to get back.

"But, what about our plans to go to the palace?" she asked.

"Some other time," he said firmly.

"Listen, Arjuna," Ulupi said as he was about to leave.

Arjuna stopped and turned around.

Ulupi was fidgeting with her hands, nervous. "Arjuna, I have to confess something to you, something I've meant to say for a long time," she said "I have been following you since the day you got here and the reason is that I find you very attractive. Since the first day, I have been only thinking about you. I just want to be with you. I want you."

Arjuna didn't know what to say.

"I'm sorry, I know this is a big surprise for you," she said. "I know you need time to understand it. I have reached a stage where I am desperate to be with you. I want you as my husband. Please marry me. I love you."

These sentences came as a shock to Arjuna. He couldn't digest them all. She seemed too desperate for him and it was scary. It felt like she was ready to do anything to have him and from his experience he knew that the most dangerous people were the ones who were desperate. That made Ulupi a dangerous person. He had to be careful with his words. He wanted to reject the proposal as it didn't make any sense. They hardly knew each other and he was married already. But also, he didn't want to break her heart and make her feel embarrassed.

He said, "First of all, I would like to say that you are the most attractive woman I have ever seen in my life. But I am on a pilgrimage here; my journey is more about self-development and understanding. I want to become a better person than before. So, it wouldn't be very appropriate if I...married someone. Now isn't the right time. I'm sorry. Marriage would add a different meaning to my trip."

Ulupi was deeply disappointed. She looked down at the floor and didn't speak for a few minutes.

"Is it because I am a Naga?" she asked.

"No, it has nothing to do with who we are or our families," Arjuna said. "In fact, I love the Nagas more than my own tribe. It's not that, it's us. We barely know each other. We simply can't marry each other just because we are two good-looking people who are physically attracted. It would be very silly of us."

"Why not?" she asked, defiant. "We can marry for whatever reason we choose. It doesn't matter."

She was right in a way. There was no reason why they couldn't marry each other, there were many couples who had married just out of attraction and ended up leading happy married lives.

"Listen, it is not you. *I* don't want to marry anyone. *I'm* not in the right mental space to be with someone. I'm sorry," Arjuna said.

Ulupi was on the verge of tears.

He left her there and returned to his hut.

15

The Underwater World

The sweet sounds of the forest couldn't wake him and he overslept that day. Once he was awake, he went to collect food. He was thinking of Ulupi and he felt bad for her. He would have said yes to her under different circumstances. He was on a pilgrimage and there was Draupadi to consider as well. When he got back to his hut, he saw Ulupi standing there, waiting for him. Arjuna didn't know why she was back, to show him her palace or to convince him to marry her.

Ulupi said, "Are you ready to come to my palace?"

Even though he was in no mood to see the palace, he was relieved that Ulupi didn't plan on pestering him about marriage. He would end their brief encounter by visiting her palace. "This is the last time we are going to meet," Arjuna warned her. "Please try and understand that I am taking up only this invite. And besides, I will be leaving early morning tomorrow."

"Fine by me. All that matters is that you are coming with me now," Ulupi said.

It was a quiet walk, most of the way. Ulupi tried her best to draw him out by asking questions about his experiences in the forest, but she received brief replies. He wasn't in the mood for talk and Ulupi let him be quiet for some time. Late in the morning, they reached the riverbank. Ulupi stood near the water, looking at it like she was examining the flow of the currents and the depth of the river.

"Are we going to swim across? It looks deep and I really don't feel comfortable. Maybe I should head back to my hut," Arjuna said.

"Come on, it's not going to harm you," Ulupi begged.

Arjuna was feeling sorry for her. She had to keep persuading him and put up with his tantrums. He knew she was too beautiful for him, she could have had any prince in this world, but she kept chasing after him even after being rejected.

"Okay, we have to swim then," Arjuna said.

"I know this will sound crazy to you, but it's possible. You have to trust me on this," she said as she slowly placed one foot in the water.

"What is it?"

"Have you heard stories about underwater palaces and how we Nagas build our entire kingdoms underground?"

"Yes..." And it dawned on him. Her palace was under water. How would they get there? And how was it possible to build anything under water?

"We the Nagas build our palaces under water and that is where we live," she said breezily. "Don't be shocked. We are powerful creatures and we have powers that no one else in the world possesses. We are the best..." She was showing off and also reminding Arjuna how powerful she actually was. If she wanted, she could use any of her Naga powers on him.

"That's really interesting. So, you can breathe underwater with your special powers but what about me?" he asked.

Ulupi laughed out loud on hearing this. "Don't be so skeptical about me. Trust me and hold my hand," she said calmly. She slowly took Arjuna's hand. He reluctantly let her.

Ulupi started walking to the water with Arjuna. He didn't know what to expect. The water was warm, perfect for a swim. They walked till the water was upto their necks.

"Well now, it's getting really deep," he panicked.

Ulupi turned to Arjuna and smiled. "Don't worry, just a deep breath, the deepest you possibly can," she said.

"I don't think that is going to be…"

"Take a deep breath. Do as I say for once. Nothing will happen to you. Trust me," she interrupted him.

He took the deepest breath and held it in. He had done breath-holding training exercises before and his maximum timing was five minutes. Bhim's was the highest at ten minutes, he was really good in the water. But that was a long time ago, when Arjuna was at the peak of his training. So, he could go to about two, three minutes now if his lungs were good enough.

Ulupi dipped her head into the water and submerged herself. Arjuna was pulled down along with her. He couldn't see clearly. The water was filled with plants and dust. Fishes brushed past him as he floated with her. His vision slowly improved. He was in the underwater world now. He saw plenty of colourful fishes swimming. Close to Ulupi and him was a huge school of big, dark-blue fishes swimming together in a whirlpool. The sunlight which penetrated through the water reflected off their skins giving off a glow. A small red-and-white striped fish swam past his face.

Ulupi had very few clothes on, just a blouse and a mini-dhoti. He skins cells had metamorphised to scales, illuminating the blue water with golden rays. Even her face and her nose had flattened a lot; she had no nose, just two nostrils in its place. Her eyes were extended further to the sides of her head. This was her true Naga avatar. Arjuna realised he wasn't feeling breathless. Ulupi had transferred her powers temporarily to him. Even he was part Naga now; his skin had become rough and scaly too.

Ulupi swam freely, enjoying herself as usual. First, she pushed herself deep into the river, touched the bottom, and rose up slowly, small bubbles coming out of her nostrils as she swam. She circled around Arjuna a couple of times, encouraging him to loosen up a little. He first tried to float in his space itself, taking some time to master the technique of swimming underwater, but with the temporary powers bestowed upon him by Ulupi, just a little push of his legs or hands would propel him for a long distance. He couldn't control his direction in the beginning but soon realised that his hands and legs helped him navigate the water.

He swam around a bit: it was the most peaceful yet exciting swim of his life. The complete underwater silence, the colourful fishes and fauna...aquatic life mesmerised him. He decided to enjoy his time underwater. Ulupi was happy to see him happy. She swam across and held out her hand. She would head to the palace with him. This time, Arjuna didn't hesitate to hold her. They swam ahead and went deeper into the river. It was getting darker, the deeper they went. There were many huge rock formations and stones on the bed of the river. It looked almost like an ocean bed down there. In a while they reached a gateway cave.

16

The Naga Palace

The cave was a huge, uneven structure, which was formed from millions of years of stone deposition. It had a narrow opening through which they had to pass. This was a passage only for the Nagas. No ordinary man could survive in it.

Ulupi went first, Arjuna followed her. The cave was pitch dark. They had special vision to tackle it. In the interiors of the cave, Arjuna noticed deadly animals along the walls, ready to attack. The Nagas had a good alliance with the reptiles and water snakes. The main protectors of the cave were the water snakes and poisonous flora. From the middle of the cave, there came the light from beautiful, brightly-coloured plants, which attracted Arjuna to them. He wanted one so he went closer to touch it, but Ulupi pulled his hand back and wagged her finger indicating to him not to touch them. They were poisonous.

The bright light blinded him for a few seconds before he saw the mystic Naga palace in front of him. It was constructed entirely on the river bottom and he was dazzled by the sight. He had visited a lot of places and kingdoms, but this one he considered to be better than Indraprastha. On land, Indraprastha was the best, but in water, this had no competition. They swam close to the huge golden structure which reflected sunlight in the day and moonlight at night.

The whole palace was in laid out in blocks, but not symmetrical ones. It looked uneven and irregular but the structure had been stable since two centuries. The topmost block which was the widest and the largest, carried the Naga deity's image. It was made of heavy grey stone and had five heads all attached to each other. The heads fanned out, the eyes were made of dark green jewels which reflected the light. The tongues protruded.

Ulupi guided him towards the structure. As they swam, she told him tales of its construction and legacy. Inside the palace premises, they could even talk underwater. The water there could transmit the voice frequencies of the Nagas.

"It is the most beautiful thing I have ever seen in my entire life," he said. It was a dream come true for a person like him who loved art and architecture.

"I told you won't regret it. You don't look like you are in a hurry to get back to your hut," Ulupi mocked him.

Arjuna smiled as he accepted defeat. "Thank you for this honour, and I am really sorry about the way I treated you. I was consumed by myself and yet you have let me into your lovely palace. I can't tell you how much I respect you for this."

"Don't worry about it," Ulupi smiled at him and kept swimming.

They swam around the palace, enjoying all the pieces of art and their beauty.

"The construction of this palace would have been very difficult at the time," he said. "The whole thing was constructed underground itself. Or was it built on land and later flooded with water, which seems to be the more reasonable option? I can't imagine building the whole thing underwater."

"It was done completely underwater, and yes, it was a long, tedious task," she said. "At the time my people faced a lot of complications and difficulties, but finally they got it done. Only the Nagas could do it. Actually, my great grandfather was the one who looked after the construction. Just a handful of members of the Airavat clan dared to do this and look what they achieved."

"Yes, surely only the Nagas are capable of such an impossible task." Arjuna had thought that the Pandavas were the best builders in the country but now he realised that the greatest architects were indeed the Nagas.

"Sadly, our population is under severe threat from the hunters and other kingdoms," Ulupi said. "I don't know where our future is headed. Our special powers have caught the attention of big kingdoms like yours. Kings and princes find themselves vulnerable and weak in front of us, so, they want to eliminate us using all their power and money. We can fight back, but we are the last generation of the Airavat clan and we don't want to risk our lives for no reason. Right now, we are trying to hide from the outside world, but I don't know how long we will be able to survive."

Arjuna sympathised with her, but he knew this was how the world worked. Nobody likes change and when the wealthy and the powerful see someone else rising to the top, they use all kinds of methods to crush those at the bottom of the ladder. Arjuna decided to change the topic and talk about more pleasant things. He spotted a few buildings around the palace. Only Ulupi, her father and their family stayed at the palace. Some of the companions of the clan stayed in the neighbouring structures. And more construction was being planned.

Ulupi started swimming away from the palace, towards the horizon.

"Where are we going? Is there anything else you want to show me?" Arjuna asked.

"Yes," she said. "My favourite part of the palace is further away. Once you see it, it's going to be your favourite as well."

Ulupi and Arjuna swam ahead till Arjuna spotted a small structure. He guessed this was her favourite. This small, isolated cave-like structure stood all by itself. There was no flora and fauna around it. It was unusual in every sense. A brownish white cave with an opening just big enough to allow Ulupi to pass through. There was only one entrance and from the outside, it looked like only Ulupi could fit into that space.

"Trust me, it's bigger than it looks," she said with a playful smile.

Arjuna had no reason not to trust her this time. Ulupi entered the cave first. On entering, Arjuna was blinded by the light. Then, his eyes adjusted to the bright stream of light.

17

Ulupi's Chambers

The cave was Ulupi's personal chamber. Inside it was a huge, well-furnished room. The room was well kept and it smelt great. The fragrance came from the aquatic flora. The walls of the room filtered the water and extracted the fragrance which was then sprayed into the room in small, regular quantities. The actual material of the walls was kept a secret by the Nagas.

The interiors were completely antique. There were several statues and paintings in the room. The paintings were all of sensuous Naga women. In one, an attractive woman was having a bath in a river with her friends, and it reminded Arjuna of the first time he saw Ulupi. Another was a portrait of a Naga woman, her head shaven, her green eyes tapering outwards, her upper body bare, revealing round, big breasts. Her abdomen was flat, but her lower body tapered off like a snake's tail. There were sculptures adorned with precious stones as well. Arjuna admired all the art on display in the cave.

"Do you like it? This is my favourite, most personal space. Away from the palace," Ulupi said as she moved closer to the mirror. She was back to her human form, but she was dripping with water.

"It is stunning," Arjuna said, examining the room closely.

"It's the place I always come to when I feel bored or want some time for myself. It helps me think and relax," Ulupi said, letting her blouse fall to the ground. Her back was bare, but her hair was let down and it covered her breasts. She didn't put on her new clothes. She just stood there looking at the mirror. She waited for a reaction from Arjuna.

Arjuna turned away, but he ended up looking at her after a few minutes.

"You should change into a fresh pair of clothes," she said, handing him a cotton dhoti.

Arjuna hesitated, then, accepted her offer.

Ulupi giggled. "It's fine, don't worry," she said. "There is no one else in here and I don't mind you looking at me. I am totally comfortable in your presence. Besides it's not like you haven't seen me in this avatar before. Remember the river with my friends?"

Arjuna was just pretending to not want to see her beauty. He would have married her by now if not for his pilgrimage. He wondered if Ulupi could be an exception to his philosophy. Ulupi slowly stood up and came over to him. She looked fresh and beautiful, her thin, curvy hips swayed from side to side as she moved. Her green eyes shone. Arjuna loved her smell, it was exotic, and something he had never breathed in before. She came closer and closer and stopped right next to him, breathing on his face and waiting for his response. He was getting very nervous, he turned his head away. He closed his eyes.

"Don't pretend you don't want this," Ulupi whispered in his ear. "I know we both want the same thing. I am asking you again. Please, marry me. You won't regret it."

Arjuna had to make a decision. Either stick to his word or accept her as his wife, either his philosophy or her beauty. He couldn't think clearly. Ulupi was too lovely for him to reject. He made his choice.

"I will marry you," he said and kissed her without waiting for her reply. He wrapped his arms around her and pulled her close.

This alliance with the Nagas would turn out to be very fruitful for the Pandava Prince. In fact, Ulupi would prove to be more useful than all his other wives.

"Tonight, I will enlighten you in ways you have never imagined. You will learn everything you seek from this pilgrimage in one night," Ulupi whispered, giving him a passionate kiss. "We will get married tomorrow in the palace. My father will be happy to hear that you are going to be his son-in-law."

Arjuna smiled at her.

"You will not continue your pilgrimage, right?" Ulupi asked.

"I really want to continue my travels," he said. "That has been my dream ever since I was a trained warrior. But don't worry about that now. This is our moment. Let's enjoy it."

He didn't want to think about leaving her. He was in love again.

18

Arjuna's Second Marriage

The next day, Ulupi told her father about her marriage plans. A grand ceremony was arranged in the underwater palace. It was a private affair with only a select few invited. The Airavat clan didn't want to show off and attract unwanted attention. Kauravya knew that the alliance between a Pandava and a Naga would spark controversy and lead to opposition from both groups.

Arjuna and Ulupi were greeted with great fanfare by the Nagas. Arjuna was surprised by the warmth and hospitality of the Airavat clan and the Nagas. The marriage to Ulupi gave him unlimited underwater powers, and absolute control over the underwater world. He could even control the flora and aquatic animals. Arjuna had become the king of the underwater realm. Master of land and water.

For a week after their marriage, Ulupi and Arjuna went for their daily morning baths together to the spot where they first met. That was the place closest to their hearts. Ulupi walked to the water, slowly undressing along the way. Arjuna watched from the shore, tempted to join her in the water. No mortal could resist Ulupi's charms and her sensuous body. She gathered her hair and slung it on her right shoulder, exposing her back. She turned around slightly and gave him one of her most inviting smiles. Arjuna remembered the thrill of the previous night they had spent together. Ulupi was the most beautiful creature on earth. She was pure magic and he was so glad he had married her.

Ulupi stood still when the water was upto her hips, her back to Arjuna. He stood there watching her shining brown skin. He was a lucky man to have her for his wife. Arjuna noticed the black mole on the side of her hips, just above the curve of her buttocks. Ulupi splashed water on herself, doing it at her own pace, waiting for Arjuna to pounce on her. Even though she could have initiated their lovemaking, she didn't. She wanted to tempt Arjuna and let him make the first move. This would show that he was more desperate than her and give her control. She loved to be in charge and always got what she wanted.

Arjuna slowly entered the water. The sun shone on the water and warmed it up. He didn't rush. He never did that with Draupadi and now with Ulupi. Letting the anticipation build up was a good thing in his book. Ulupi pulled him closer, her breathing steadily rising. Arjuna was known all over the land as a master of the stringed weapon and a great warrior, but more importantly, he was a perceptive lover. He showered the women he loved with attention.

The current was strong and before he knew it, his dhoti was stripped away by the river. Arjuna stood right behind Ulupi. He breathed in her exotic smell which made him lightheaded with excitement. He brushed his lips against her cheeks. The water had made her skin even softer than it was. When he kissed the nape of her neck, she moaned. His hands slid down from her shoulders to her smooth arms and to her curvy hips. He smelled her hair again, and kissed her shoulders. Her dhoti had been washed away by the water. Arjuna started kissing her back, his hands still on her hips. He kissed her all over, his grip on her waist tightened, and he was now squeezing her smooth, soft flesh. He tasted the water on her back. He loved the taste of her skin.

His lips touched the mole on her hip and Ulupi sighed. She stood there, eyes half closed, eager for his kisses. He wanted the two of them to stay like this forever. His hands lingered on her body, her waist, her thighs, her perfect round breasts. Arjuna put his hands on her shoulders and slowly turned her around to face him. Her breath caressed his face. He pressed her hips close to his body. Ulupi shuddered with anticipation. A much-awaited kiss was on the way.

19

Arjuna's Departure

Arjuna and Ulupi spent a few intensely romantic weeks together. They bathed in the mornings, dried themselves and lolled around on the banks of the river in the sun. They basked in the warmth of each other's company. The time came when Arjuna decided that he would be leaving soon. He was not ready to stop his journey here. He wanted to keep going, but he would not leave without telling Ulupi his plans and break her heart. He had hurt Draupadi when he left home and he was not going to make the same mistake with Ulupi.

"Ulupi," Arjuna said gently.

Ulupi was resting her head on his shoulder.

"Yes," she said, without taking her eyes off the water.

"I need to tell you something. It might hurt you, but I'm going to come out and say it," he said.

Ulupi was suddenly alert. She looked at him. "Is it about your solo travels?" she asked.

He was relieved that he didn't have to deliver the message himself.

"What are you saying?" she asked, agitated. "I won't let you go. You said you would stay. You promised."

"Ulupi...Ulupi," Arjuna shushed her and let her rest her head on his shoulders. He let her cry for a few minutes. "Listen," he said. "As much as I want to stay here with you, my travels are important to me. This has been the purpose of my trip. I am so lucky to have met you and if I continue my travels, I will learn more and meet new people. Don't you want your husband to become a better person? The best warrior? Think about it, when I return I will be a better lover to you and a better husband."

Ulupi didn't know what to say, she just sat there very quietly.

"Ulupi, as you know a warrior needs to continuously train, learn and acquire knowledge. And that is exactly what I am doing. Please, I need your support on this," Arjuna pleaded.

Ulupi took a few seconds to respond. "I would never let you leave," she sobbed. "But I also care about what you want and your goals. Promise me you will be back as soon as you can. I can't live without you for long"

"I promise I will be back soon. Sooner than you know. Thank you, Ulupi, for understanding me. I love you," Arjuna said, holding her close. "You are a strong woman with special powers to change the world. Take care of yourself and help others to live a good life. I will join you soon."

The next day, he packed all his belongings, his tent, his cloth, his bow and arrows, and the food provided by Ulupi. Arjuna had three backpacks to carry on his shoulder. One was food, the next were the folded-up tents and the third, his weaponry. He had prepared for a long walk for the next month. He was going to the north-eastern part of the country. It was a long and exciting journey.

Ulupi was there to wish him goodbye. She had helped him with the packing too. She had a parting gift for him, a special arrow that was not made of metal or wood. It was fashioned out of a flexible rubber-like material, twisting and curling like a serpent, the sharp end in the shape of the head of a Naga with a protruding red tongue acting as the sharpest point.

"This is very special," she said. "I have to give it to you before you leave. This arrow was first made by the first Naga and it has been blessed by Lord Shiva. It was used by all the previous generations of my family and now I want you to have it. You are worthy of it."

Arjuna accepted the latest and the most powerful addition to his collection of arrows. He now had arrows of metal, wood, stone and snake skin.

"Once you have used the arrow, it will come back to you," Ulupi said. "It is yours forever. This is the most powerful arrow of the Naga kingdom. So, take care of it and respect it. It will do you much good."

Arjuna took the arrow and touched both of his eyes with it, asking for blessings.He hugged Ulupi for the last time before leaving.

"Take care of yourself," she said, wiping away her tears.

Chitrangada

20

Manipur, Arjuna's Next Destination

The journey was long but very pleasant for Arjuna. He was used to travelling by now. He followed the same daily routine. He walked till sunset, then, assembled his makeshift tent and found a spot for sleeping. He had no worries regarding food because Ulupi had given him a surplus supply. It could last for twice the length of the journey. But Arjuna still tried collecting fruits and wood. He didn't want to miss out on the essential experience of survival in the forest.

He only bathed once a week and kept his beard long and knotted. He stayed mostly along the banks of the Ganges. He wanted to stay near the river but if he was planning on venturing to the deep north-eastern parts, he had to let go of the river for some time. The river would re-emerge later and then drain in the east. In order to cover a few weeks of dry land, he had to survive on the water he had collected on his way. It was difficult but he managed to pull it off. Some small lakes and freshwater bodies helped him get through this patch.

When he reached the northeast, he was amazed at the beauty of this unexplored part. It was the most ignored part of the country mostly because of geographical reasons. The majority of the prominent kingdoms were in the north and the south, the rest of them were mostly small, and scattered all over. The northeast had only one kingdom. The palace was situated in Manipur and King Chitravahana was famous for his kindness and his well-maintained relationships with most kingdoms. He had an exceptional and long-lasting relationship with Hastinapur. He loved the Pandavas.

Not just the Manipur Kingdom, the whole of the north was known for its natural beauty. The geography was mesmerising. It was a place of valleys and mountains with a lot of greenery. The climate was diverse as well. In the early morning the sky was covered with fog and the temperatures dropped, some parts had heavy rain whereas others were dry. The culture was a rich and varied one. Arjuna was enjoying his time here. He had already forgotten Ulupi.

King Chitravahana had promoted the northeast all his life and he loved his kingdom more than anything else in the world. He had only one daughter, Chitrangandha. He was eager to find a suitable prince to marry her off to. Arjuna was just outside the Kingdom of Manipur in a small village at the time. There was only a small colony of about 15 huts there and very few people. Arjuna had made friends with the children who lived there. He enjoyed their company and felt compelled to stay for a few weeks because of them.

That noon, Arjuna had just finished a heavy, delicious lunch. He had taken an hour to finish the typical northeaster, liquid soft rice with a red gravy, which was a burst of spices and flour. There were three or four varieties of vegetables cut up into small pieces and mixed up with spices, acting as small bites. Then came the sweet treats, semi-liquid sugar rice pudding, solid brown laddoos and pomegranate juice. It was a warm and pleasant afternoon. After taking some rest, he started playing with a four year old. The child, the son of the owners of the house he was staying at, was trying to build something with sticks and sand. Arjuna sat beside him and admired him. The dog joined in. The boy, the cutest child Arjuna had ever seen, took a stick and offered it to Arjuna with his small hands. Arjuna couldn't decline the offer from someone so innocent. He took the stick and attached it firmly in line with his previous stick. The boy smiled. His hands and face were covered in sand.

Arjuna liked the children in this village because they grew up in a very peaceful and natural manner. No one forced them to do anything unlike in the other kingdoms where they had to learn archery and other skills for waging wars. Children were taught how to kill people at a young age. Arjuna felt they must be allowed to live their childhood freely, in harmony.

The boy got bored of the sticks and sand and started playing with the dog. He rolled over the dog and the dog obliged. They were the perfect example of innocence. They were not tainted by greed or want of material possessions. Arjuna knew he was guilty of this fault, but he considered himself to be somewhat better than his cousins, the Kauravas. After a while, the boy's mother walked up to them. It was bath time for him. The boy saw his mother and suddenly sat upright as if he wasn't playing in the sand at all. The mother was carrying her second child. The baby was just a few months old and was suspended from a sack made of cloth and tied to her shoulders. Arjuna respected her a lot. She made him feel at home and took good care of him.

Arjuna looked at the baby and made a funny face which didn't seem to affect her. She continued sucking her thumb. Arjuna couldn't control himself, he wanted to pull the baby's cheeks. He could resist Ulupi's charms but not this baby's cuteness, not even once. He pulled her cheeks, they were soft as cotton and wobbled at his touch.

The mother kissed her daughter on her cheeks. She loved her children very much.

"These are the cutest children I have ever seen," Arjuna said.

"Yes, very cute but they are naughty as well. It is no easy task looking after them," she said.

"And I hope Rigi hasn't troubled you much. He is a little troublemaker at times," the mother continued with a laugh. The dog stood next to the boy wagging his tail. The dog and the boy were best friends.

"Not at all, it was my pleasure to spend time with him," Arjuna said.

"He's very sweet in the beginning but once he gets comfortable with you, you really don't know the trouble he can create," she said, wiping the sweat off her forehead.

It must be terrible for her to handle two small kids, one a naughty boy and the other a baby girl. Arjuna knew she was in trouble. He wondered how his mother Kunti must have managed her five little Pandavas.

"I hope you are comfortable in the house. Please ask me if you need anything," the mother said.

Arjuna was provided with a room in their hut and he was treated like a king. They made him the best food they could offer and didn't let him experience any difficulty. He hadn't experienced such comfort in his own palace. In Indraprastha, he always dressed formally to attend court meetings and training sessions and he could only be himself inside his room. It felt like he was controlled by someone else every minute of his day. But here, he could do whatever he wanted.

"No problem at all," he said. "You have been very kind to me. I pray that your children grow up to be great people."

The mother smiled. "I hope so too," she said.

"I am thinking of moving on. Tomorrow I will be leaving for Manipur," he told her.

"Good luck to you. And don't worry about the food, I will pack the food and water for your journey," she promised.

"Thank you," said a grateful Arjuna.

The woman saw that her son was covered in mud. She tried to scrape some of it off his face with her hands, but the mud had become too dry. "If you don't mind, I have to give him a proper wash. He has made a mess," she said, dragging Rigi along to the well. Arjuna saw the boy putting his tongue out and laughing as he was torturing his poor mother.

The mother had already prepared warm water and kept it ready. She poured the water over Rigi and the child started jumping up and down, enjoying his bath. Rigi turned back and waved at Arjuna when his mother was drying him after his bath.

The best child ever, Arjuna thought. He considered taking Rigi with him to Indraprastha, training him and giving him a good position in the army. But then he realised that if he did so, he would be taking away the child's freedom. So, he decided to offer him an education or training of his choice when he grew up. Arjuna could stay with Rigi the rest of the year, but he had to travel and see more of the country. Like he had told Ulupi, he would meet many more good people along the way. He just had to move on. He wondered if Draupadi had learnt to live without him. Ulupi would be desperately waiting for his return.

Early the next day, Arjuna bid goodbye to Rigi, his parents, his baby sister and the dog. He would honour them for their service once he was back at Indraprastha.

21

The Kingdom of Manipur

When Arjuna reached Manipur, he was astounded by the city's blend of natural and man-made structures. For the past few months, he had been living in the woods and so the kingdom appeared more beautiful to him. It was almost as good as Indraprastha but smaller in terms of size. Unlike in most other kingdoms, the main palace was not situated at the centre. It stood on the extreme edge, just before the entry gate of the nearest kingdom.

Arjuna didn't understand the logic of risking the main palace to an attack by the enemy. But then, King Chitravahana was known for his selfless nature. He was a warrior and his army was famous for its well-trained, but artistically inclined soldiers. The soldiers of Manipur could fight with their bare hands, sticks, swords, bows, knives and other weapons. They were the masters of martial arts. They weren't taking a risk by placing the palace at the border. They were well prepared and always on alert to fight any army that threatened their kingdom.

Arjuna walked up to a man selling fresh coconut water and bought some for himself. He took a big gulp of the fresh coconut water. As he was finishing his drink, he heard a group of men talking close by. They looked worried.

"It's sad, now who will take the lead?" one of the men asked. "Who is going to train the soldiers and carry out the responsibility? Our whole army was dependent on him and there is no future king to bank on. It will be difficult for Princess Chitrangada to handle the situation all by herself."

A second man replied, "He served us for so many years and now, it's going to be difficult for King Chitravahana and Chitrangada to handle the situation. Our kingdom will be in crisis soon. Our only strength was the army...and now this...We'll also see the economic crisis getting worse."

Manipur's main revenue came from the various alliances with other kingdoms. The Manipur Kingdom offered high-end, trained security services in the form of soldiers and military equipment to others and made a fortune. However, in the past year, they had faced some serious competition from the south. The south also started making their own equipment and selling them, that too at a cheaper rate. Manipur still controlled a majority share of the security services market in the country mainly due to the quality of its soldiers and their reputation, but it had suffered a major blow to its income in the past year. The kingdom had to spend a lot of money on marketing its equipment to prospective buyers and it was approaching crisis mode now. A very difficult time indeed!

"Manipur's future doesn't look very bright," said one of the men. "I hope King Chitravahana will find a successor soon. He desperately needs a man to marry off his daughter to. There has to be an heir to the throne."

They chatted about Manipur's crisis for some more time and Arjuna took in all the information. In the end, they agreed that only the King could solve this problem.

Arjuna asked the coconut vendor casually. "Is there a major problem that has affected the people? Why is everyone so unhappy today?"

"Aren't you from here?" the vendor asked, cutting open a coconut right at the centre. He used both his hands and with brute force, tore it into two parts.

"I am just a traveller," Arjuna said.

"So, you are travelling through Manipur? Good. I am eager to travel across the country. One day, I will save enough money and do it"

Arjuna wasn't interested in what he wanted to do.

"Manipur is in a difficult phase right now," the vendor said. "The army's top General met with an unfortunate accident today, during one of their training sessions. The elephant he was riding went wild and caused a riot in the army academy ground and the General was crushed under the elephant's foot. He was the only victim. The whole city is devastated. He was a good man and people respected him a lot."

Arjuna digested this news as he ate the tender coconut flesh the vendor handed him. It tasted like sweet, flavoured, thick milk.

"The General was in charge of training the army all these years. Without him, the King and the Princess will find it tough to recruit new soldiers. The army is getting old and needs younger and stronger recruits. The only way out is for the King to appoint a new General. A big decision has to be made," the vendor said. He was in the mood to talk and Arjuna was the last customer of the day.

Arjuna understood Manipur's situation clearly. The people of Manipur were worried about their future. He thanked the vendor and headed for the palace. He wanted to meet King Chitravahana.

22

Arjuna Meets King Chitravahana

Arjuna stayed at a house not far from the palace after paying a hefty rent that night. Due to the bad economy, people were charging high prices for every service. The next day, he went straight to the palace.

Arjuna stood right in front of the huge palace which looked more like a military base. There were soldiers everywhere, some of them on duty, some marching, and some just killing time. The palace consisted of two pointed structures projecting out to the sky and diverging from each other. The base was one single solid, from which the two structures were projected. There was a central gap in between the two with plenty of crawlers. This gave the palace a unique and outdoor-like look. There was a circle of plants and small trees just around the base. Wherever there was an inch of empty space, one could see greenery. It was an amazing showcase of the mix of nature and human creativity.

Arjuna could not find the entrance at the front. So, he circled around the palace. As he started walking, he saw the very visible transition from a civilian palace to an army base. Behind the palace was where the army base was located. Soldiers lived and trained here.

Arjuna liked the idea of a combined palace and army base but he also thought that this arrangement would limit the privacy of the royals. He noticed the palace premises were overcrowded with outsiders and army personnel. Arjuna took a short tour of the army base and it made him realise how much King Chitravahana and the people of Manipur valued their army and security. The army base was massive and it was built like a solid square block. The soldiers were constantly moving in and out of it. The main door was shared by the palace and the base, but there was a smaller gateway on the side that led directly to the palace. He guessed this was reserved for the royals who did not want to mix with the army.

Arjuna was wearing his usual cream-coloured dhoti. He had been using it since the beginning of the trip. He also had a backpack of cloth which hung across his shoulders. He had only two dhotis and he used one of them as an angavastram when needed.

He approached the gatekeeper. "My name is Arjuna," he said. "I have come from Indraprastha and to meet King Chitravahana. I am a good friend of his. Can you let him know I am here?"

The gatekeeper scanned Arjuna from top to bottom. He kept a straight face and replied, "Visiting hours does not start till tomorrow afternoon and there is a long queue of appointments before you. I advise you to come back tomorrow or wait for your turn. There is no special entry for anyone."

Arjuna wasn't disappointed. Manipuri soldiers were known for their discipline.

"Kindly mention my name to the King," he said.

"Please wait," pat came the reply.

Arjuna looked around and observed his surroundings. He always liked watching people and understanding their life from far. The first thing he noticed was a group of children, ranging from five to ten years old, training to get into the army. They were all arranged height-wise, the smallest ones were in front, the tallest at the back. They were learning martial arts. The main instructor kept his legs apart, half squatting, arms by his waist, and let out a loud "ah" from his epiglottis and threw a punch into the air.

A little away from them were the big boys, almost fully-trained soldiers, and the future of Manipur. This was their advanced training session and they had their weapons with them. First it was the long sticks they swung above their heads, next the swords with which they duelled each other. After that, they had to run an exhausting ten-mile obstacle course. Arjuna also spotted the veterans from the army. Anyone could tell by the looks of them that they were ready to fight, fit and well trained. All the soldiers stood in line, bowing their heads to honour their fallen teacher whose sword was displayed before them. After this, they huddled together for a tactical recoup. Arjuna remembered his previous wars. He felt the pride and the honour they were feeling at the moment.

"Sir, did you want to meet the King?" a man came up to him and asked. He looked like the palace guide.

"Yes, yes," Arjuna said.

"Please come. The King invites you to meet him. Please follow me," the man said.

Arjuna followed him through the door that led directly to the palace.

"What is the other door for?" he asked the man.

"Oh, that one is for the army. There is a separate block for army personnel and only they stay there. No one else gets access through it," the man said.

"It's the first time I have seen this sort of arrangement for the army. It's a very good one. I never thought of it before," Arjuna said.

"The King always gives special consideration to the army and Princess Chitragandha. She is more of a warrior than a princess, so every soldier gets more facilities and priorities than the top cabinet ministers. This is how our kingdom works and it has done us well. Hope it works the same way in the future," the man said.

"That's amazing," Arjuna remarked. He thought that the soldiers who dedicated their lives to the kingdom deserved respect and all facilities.

They passed through a series of at least ten doors, each bigger and wider than the one before. Finally, after walking down many corridors, they reached a small courtroom. This was the place where King Chitravahana relaxed during the mornings or after his court sessions.

"The King will be arriving shortly, please," the man said as he showed Arjuna to his seat.

Arjuna roamed around the well-furnished room after the man left. The lighting was dim. Despite the afternoon sun and soaring temperatures outside, the room felt like a cool, relaxing space. Arjuna noticed the portraits of army generals and warriors who had given their life for the kingdom hanging on the walls. He also noticed the portraits of the warrior Princess Chitrangada in various battle positions. The pictures were not detailed enough for him to discern her looks. He had to meet her in person to find out.

"Hello, my friend!"

Arjuna turned around to see King Chitravahana smiling at him. King Chitravahana was an old friend. They had been in touch when the Pandavas were staying in Hastinapur with the Kauravas. During the conflict between the two, King Chitravahana took the Pandavas's side and helped them in every way including by providing them financial support. Arjuna was really happy to meet the King after a long time. He hugged his friend and patted him on the back.

"How are you, my friend? I hope I have not made you wait for long," the King said. There was genuine concern in his eyes for Arjuna.

Arjuna smiled. He couldn't believe that he had finally managed to meet Chitravahana face to face. There was a sense of euphoria in the room.

"Come, sit. We have a lot to talk about," Chitravahana said as he sat down next to Arjuna. Usually he would sit only opposite someone, but today he was meeting his friend, so, there was no formality.

"So, you have a beard now?" the King asked fondly.

Arjuna laughed as he brushed his beard with his fingers. It had grown up to his chest.

A few servers arrived with refreshments. They kept plates of dry fruits and nuts, coconut water and juice before the King and his guest.

Arjuna munched on a couple of nuts. Then, he started to chat with the King, "I left Indraprastha a year ago on a self-imposed exile. My brothers didn't want me to leave. I needed more time for myself. I wanted to discover the world and understand how it works. The only way I can do that is if I travel and experience it myself. So, I headed out..." He didn't mention Draupadi to the King.

Chitravahana looked very interested in Arjuna's story. "Is there a problem? Can I help you with anything?" he asked.

"No, I'm not in any kind of trouble," Arjuna said.

Chitravahana was relieved and he took a big gulp of juice.

"The past six months, I have been travelling all across the country. I have learnt a lot and understood life during the time. The northeast, beautiful Manipur, is also a part of my travels," Arjuna said.

"That is very bold of you, to decide to leave your family and travel alone. It must be very exciting and satisfying. This is every man's dream...to go wherever he desires," King Chitravahana said. "I would love to do it, but it may remain a dream."

Chitravahana hadn't aged very well, he was in his early sixties now, he had a pot belly, and his knees were starting to hurt. His physical activities were much limited.

Arjuna praised him for running his kingdom so well. "You have done a fantastic job with Manipur, excellent work," he said. "I have learnt a lot from this visit. The neatness, the organisation, the well-trained army and the blend of nature and creativity in your architecture. Amazing!"

The King was delighted to receive such high praise.

"You focus a large part of your economy on the army. It's a good strategy, but why rely on the army so much?" Arjuna asked.

"We do spend a lot on the army, on weaponry and training," the King agreed. "It is because we love our army, our soldiers and our kingdom. It's our tradition. We don't have a large number of soldiers, elephants or sophisticated weapons around here, but what we have is skill, dedication and years of training. We don't want to capture other kingdoms. We are satisfied with this and allies like you as well as our army protect us from danger. We are happy in this small world of ours."

Arjuna noticed the glint of passion in his eyes when he spoke about his army.

"It's not just the soldiers who train to defend our kingdom, it's the people too," the King continued. "The people loved the army and so do I. I have been a general and served in the army. I will continue to do that," he said, his voice trailing off when he remembered he had no successor except his daughter.

"I heard about the demise of your top General," Arjuna said gently. "I'm sorry. I know Manipur is in a very delicate situation at the moment."

"Kashyap had been serving the kingdom since the beginning of my rule. He oversaw training for three generations and now we have lost a great teacher and warrior. I don't know what to do now. My daughter is doing her best to run things, but it's difficult at times," Chitravahana said sadly.

Arjuna let Chitravahana recover. After a few minutes of silence, Chitravahana refilled his glass.

Arjuna spoke up. "Actually, I have come to offer my services," he said. "The people of Manipur and you deserve better and I will do whatever it takes to get your kingdom back on its feet."

Chitravahana looked up at his friend. This was great news!

"With your permission I would like to teach archery to your special units, I will make sure they all learn all that archery has to offer. I will train them till you find someone to replace me. I can act as the interim general if you like," Arjuna said.

The King spoke after a pause. His face had fallen. "I really appreciate your concern for me and the whole of Manipur," he said. "But I don't think the rest of the cabinet will accept an outsider as Army General. It has been a long tradition that only the people who train with the Manipuris can take that post. But maybe I can try and convince my daughter and the rest…It seems like a reasonable idea to me."

Chitravahana thought about the situation deeply. The crisis was getting worse by the day. He needed to do something quickly and he was lucky enough that his friend had offered him a solution. A great warrior like Arjuna could do so much good. This was a chance too good to miss.

The King called for his palace guide, Raga. "Show Arjuna to his room and attend to his every need," he ordered.

Arjuna smiled and accepted his friend's offer to stay at the palace. There would be a cabinet meeting the next day. The King would formally propose the idea of Arjuna taking up the post of General there.

"Sir, let me show you to your room," Raga said.

Arjuna let him lead the way.

23

The Warrior Princess

Arjuna's room was on the top floor and so was King Chitravahana's. Raga escorted him there and left after helping him to settle down. The room was a simple and comfortable space with a bed and a bathroom. There was a dining table too and all the food he would require was laid out on it.

Arjuna walked to the window and looked out. The army was out there in its full strength, marching and training. It was a spectacular sight. 15,000 trained personnel were marching in sync. His eyes rested on a woman who was sword fighting at the far end. She did not wear any protective gear. It was dangerous but that was how Princess Chitrangada trained. Arjuna had heard many stories about how Chitrangada put her body on the line for simple training tasks. She was a fearless warrior goddess.

Chitrangada had short hair, shorter than Arjuna's. She was wearing a full-sleeved cream-coloured cloth which was body fitting. This was the cloth soldiers wore under their steel armour, but she wore no armour. Her full ankle-length leggings were tight.

Arjuna didn't understand how she could fight in such an uncomfortable dress. It surely must restrict her free movement, but he was happy because the dress clearly showcased her perfect body. Draupadi was beautiful, Ulupi had a curvaceous figure, but Chitrangada had both. She was athletic but not too skinny. The dress highlighted the well-shaped round contours of her breasts. Her abdomen was flat and her waist, size zero. Long legs, strong, thick thighs and muscular calves.

Chitrangada was fighting with another soldier as part of their practice session. Around them stood all the other soldiers and guards as spectators, in a circle. The match was very intense. The crowd loved their Princess and cheered for her. Chitrangada was ready to attack. She leaned forward, sword perfectly aligned along her face and pointing at her opponent. Her knees were slightly bent as she circled around and waited for an opening to strike. Her opponent, a soldier with a sword, was standing upright and moving away from the Princess. They circled a few times and as she noticed that the soldier was a bit slow in his movements, she took the chance. Using her strong hamstrings and her calf she jumped up in the air and landed on the soldier with her sword. The soldier tried to swing his sword wildly but he was already down. Chitrangada was on top of him with her sword at his neck.

She won the duel.

Everybody applauded the Princess. She extended her arm to the fallen soldier who grabbed it and got up.

"Be ready the next time," she told him and patted him on the back.

Arjuna could lip-read her easily from that distance. There had been instances where his lip-reading skills helped him win wars. Arjuna was so good at it that he could lip-read his opponents discussing their strategy from a distance and capitalise on it. He saw a lady running to the Princess with some water. From what he could see, the lady was pointing at a small wound Chitrangada had sustained from the sword, a cut on her arm, where the cloth was torn and blood was dripping. The young lady quickly cleaned the wound and applied some medicine there. Chitrangada didn't seem to care; in fact, she had not even noticed it until her faithful helper told her about it.

This impressed Arjuna very much. She didn't care about battle scars; she only cared about her kingdom. Arjuna had met many women, but none who didn't care about their looks. Arjuna loved Chitrangada for her attitude. She was different from other women...After the crowd left and Chitrangada headed back, Arjuna settled down in his room, unpacked his stuff, made himself comfortable and took a long nap. It was court day tomorrow.

24

Arjuna Appointed Manipur's Army General

The next day, fresh after a long, undisturbed sleep he got ready, wore his new white plain dhoti and a white angavastram. He also trimmed his beard and cut his hair. He looked smart and fit for the role of General. He then headed for the private court session where only important people met. King Chitravahana had called for a gathering to introduce the new General. Once it was discussed, the news would be shared with the loyal public.

All the cabinet members were already seated. Arjuna smiled at them with no reciprocation. He sat next to King Chitravahana's chair. Sensing he wasn't welcome in the discussion, he let the King commence the meeting. The King wore a golden dhoti and what looked like a heavy gold chain around his waist to secure the dhoti. A thick necklace covered most of his chest. He also wore diamond-studded earrings. He looked very regal.

Princess Chitrangada, on the other hand, was different. She didn't exactly suit the part of a beautiful princess. She looked strong and graceful, and a bit masculine. She wore a loose green cloth with floral patterns that covered her body and it was tucked in at the waist by a gold band. She wore a green dhoti along with it. Her attire was not delicately feminine. It looked to Arjuna that she was trying to make herself look like a man.

Arjuna was quick to understand why Chitrangada was hiding her beautiful feminine features. The King had no sons, and no heir to the throne. Chitrangada tried her best to convince the people of Manipur and her father that she was as good as a prince and capable of taking care of the kingdom. There was no doubt she was capable. But tradition demanded that that the true heir could only be a man and someone who was from the blood of the Manipur royal family. Either the King needed a son who he was too old to produce, or Chitrangada had to give birth to a boy. The second option was more plausible.

King Chitravahana ordered for some food to be brought in. He didn't like empty tables during meetings. He was constantly eating. "First, let me introduce all of you to Arjuna," he said as he put his arm on Arjuna's shoulder.

Arjuna acknowledged everyone and smiled at them.

"Arjuna is one of the five Pandavas, the rulers of Indraprastha," the King said. "You are wondering why I called a meeting just to introduce him? Well, we have all heard of his bravery and skills. He has a proposal in mind which he shared with me. I really liked it. I think it might be the solution to the crisis our kingdom is facing."

There was a sudden burst of chatter among the ministers. When King Chitravahana introduced Arjuna to them, none of them were excited about it. They didn't see any use for him, but now that the mention of a solution to the crisis had come up, he got everyone's attention. After a few seconds, the cabinet settled down. There was total silence once again.

"As we all know, Arjuna is a great warrior, with whom we have a wonderful alliance," the King continued. "Yesterday, he came to visit me after a long time. We spoke and he offered me something valuable, which I couldn't decline. He is ready to teach archery and impart military knowledge to our army. Therefore, I propose we make him the new interim Army General."

The cabinet ministers slowly digested the information. Most of them were happy with the offer, a few objected since Arjuna didn't belong to the Manipuri Kingdom. Also, he was a temporary option, not a long-term solution their problem. Even Princess Chitrangada hadn't been aware of the plan till that moment. She didn't know enough about Arjuna till. She needed some time to think it over. Chitravahana let them talk among themselves.

"But, Father, what about the long term prospects?" Chitrangada asked on behalf of everyone. "This doesn't solve our crisis permanently and even for now, we don't know if he is the right choice. Yes, he is a good warrior and has fought and won many battles but to lead our army is a different thing."

Arjuna was impressed with Chitrangada. She wasn't just a warrior but also a very smart woman. This was the first time Arjuna had fallen in love with a woman, but he wasn't sure if she liked him. If she had any feelings for him, she hid them well.

"Well, I'll let Arjuna answer. He is the best person to address your questions," the King said.

Arjuna stood up and greeted the gathering. "King Chitravahana and I have known each other for a long time," he said. "We Pandavas can never forget the numerous times he has helped us. I want to help him now. Apart from our close relationship, I also have formed a deep attachment to this city. I was truly amazed by its beauty and elegance. I have fallen in love with this city and the people here."

Some of the ministers looked happy with the compliments. Princess Chitrangada kept a straight face.

"And yes, coming to the most important point," Arjuna walked around the table, soaking in the attention from all the ministers. He stopped next to Chitrangada. "I recently heard about the demise of your great General," he said. "Saddened by the loss, I decided to provide temporary support and training to your army. I have a lot of experience in battle and in building armies. I will serve till you find a suitable person to lead the army. I hope you will accept me. I may be the only option you have."

Chitrangada and Arjuna stared at each other for a few seconds.

"Don't think you are the only option we have," she said. "We can manage without your assistance. Our soldiers are qualified enough."

Some of the senior ministers agreed with her. Arjuna had the majority's support but the issue was put to a vote.

"All those who don't want Arjuna to be appointed as the next General, please raise your hands," said the King.

Only a couple of hands were raised. Arjuna was surprised that Chitrangada didn't raise her hand.

"All those in favour."

The rest of the ministers raised their hands. Arjuna kept looking at Chitrangada. That was the only vote which mattered to him. She didn't raise her hand. She stayed neutral. Arjuna was disappointed with this.

King Chitravahana stood up. "Welcome to our kingdom, Arjuna," he said and gave Arjuna a hug.

Arjuna went on to shake hands with all the ministers.

Chitrangada held his hand with a firm grip. "I hope you will do justice to our army. I need you to start training them from tomorrow. All the soldiers are your responsibility as are their families and children. Manipur is your responsibility now. This is your new Indraprastha," she said.

That was cold, Arjuna thought. She was a very strong woman. He never wanted to be in her bad books.

* * *

Arjuna was shown the army headquarters that day. It was massive. He couldn't believe how big it was until he set eyes on it. There were three sections inside: the first for current soldiers, with a private chamber for the ranking men; the second was for the young beginners and all kinds of learners. The third was simply for meetings and other strategy-based discussions.

25

The First Day on the Job

Arjuna went to base early the next morning. He decided to focus on the current group of soldiers because he wanted to make sure that he got them into shape for the short term. Also, he would pick someone from the current lot to lead the army in the future.

All the soldiers were lined up before him. He saw that the strength wasn't much; it was half the size of the army of Indraprastha. Arjuna decided that it was sufficient for a small kingdom like Manipur. He didn't want to interfere with the numbers. He looked at the soldiers closely. They all looked the same physically, thin and fit, but none too strong. They didn't have the right muscular structure. He gave them a test and made them run a marathon across a distance as big as their city. They completed it easily, but when he gave them heavy weights, they couldn't handle it.

Arjuna had found one of their weaknesses. They were all good with weapons, but they lacked hand-to-hand combat skills. They didn't lift a lot of weights. Arjuna didn't want them to convert to bodybuilders but he did expect overall strength, and for that, they needed to be muscular and solid. He changed their diet plan and their workouts. They had brutal and intense exercise sessions in mornings, in the afternoons, weaponry and martial arts training, in the evenings, weight training for strength.

Strength was a key factor in battle, the benefits of which Bhim had showcased and promoted back in Indraprastha. Arjuna added more proteins to their diet and they had to eat meat now. Many resisted, but Arjuna gave them nuts as an alternative to protein. Within a month, the change was evident. The soldiers grew heavier, muscular and more flexible. Arjuna had changed their build totally. They now practised hand-to-hand combat, not just martial arts.

Since they were heavier and more powerful than before, now they lifted their opponents and threw them away, finishing the fight as quickly as possible. It took the new soldiers just three to four moves to finish their enemies, it was brutal and effective. It was no more an exchange of punches. It was way easier for them to fight and defeat the enemy now. The soldiers liked this and they respected their new guru.

Chitrangada was clearly impressed by Arjuna's training skills. He wasn't the trainer who taught what he knew best, he didn't force archery on any of the soldiers. He observed the soldiers, understood what they were missing and trained them accordingly. Chitrangada's only criterion for liking a man was that he had to be a skilled warrior. War and the kingdom was the only things she ever concentrated on, training was the only thing she did, so it was natural for her to like someone who was good at it. If Chitrangada was impressed with Arjuna's work ethic, he was totally in love with her. She was smart, a brilliant warrior and she took full responsibility for her kingdom. She truly was the best example of an independent woman.

When Arjuna finished his classes and went to watch the Princess in action, he acted as if he was just doing his rounds. Sometimes, he made his soldiers run close to the place where Chitrangada trained, so that he could see her. There were instances when he had ordered his men to do continuous runs and pushups because he was lost in his fantasies about Chitrangada and forgot the real world. The soldiers being loyal to him didn't stop till Arjuna ordered them to. They were exhausted, but Arjuna blamed them for not having enough stamina. He had to cover up his mistake!

Arjuna wanted to express his feelings for Chitrangada, but he was too scared to do it. Even with two wives, Arjuna was still scared to approach a woman. Usually women approached him. He was the one they fell for. Now he realised how difficult it was to confess one's feelings to another. He was scared to death of it. This is when he understood how much Ulupi loved him. She had pursued him inspite of his rejection.

Arjuna decided he would gather his courage and approach Chitrangada. He went to the academy to watch her train. It was an intense battle and the training session was extended more than usual. The crowd was there to watch her as always. No other part of the academy attracted so much attention; her training was entertainment for many people. Arjuna felt his chances already diminish. He knew she would be tired after the session and in no mood to talk to people. But he didn't want to wait till tomorrow.

26

Arjuna Confesses His Love

Chitrangada was resting under a tree. Arjuna observed her from a distance, he didn't want to rush. He wanted her to rest, cool down, and let her body come back to its normal state. He didn't want to talk to a warrior goddess when her body was pumped up with adrenaline, it would prove to be deadly for him!

Chitrangada sat back, extended her legs, looked at the sky and exhaled deeply. She then closed her eyes for a few seconds. Arjuna didn't want her to fall sleep. Fortunately for him, her faithful companion woke her up to clean up her wounds and to provide her with water. On seeing her companion, Chitrangada sat up straight. This showed how much she respected her helpers. She applied a green paste on her wounded leg. She closed her eyes again and let the paste dry.

Arjuna noticed her arms for the first time. They were muscular but also slender and smooth. He was falling in love with her even more every minute. He had to talk to her. He walked up to the spot where she was resting with her eyes closed.

"Hm..." Arjuna tried to wake her up by clearing his throat, but no response...He stomped his feet hard on the ground, still no response. Chitrangada's companion came up from behind and looked at him. Arjuna had completely forgotten about her.

She smiled at him, woke up Chitrangada and left. She didn't get involved in meetings. Arjuna was embarrassed but he kept smiling. Chitrangada slowly opened her eyes. She was on the verge of drifting off into a deep sleep. This was the worst time to talk to her. There was no chair to offer him, so Arjuna was left standing.

Before Arjuna could speak, she started, "Before you say anything, I have to admit you have done very impressive work with the soldiers. I can see the improvement and so can the cabinet. We are all happy with it. Just keep up your good work."

"Oh, thank you, it was my pleasure," he said, relieved she was happy with his work if not with him.

"And have you found any suitable candidate among the men to head the army?" she asked in a serious tone.

Arjuna had not even considered selecting anyone. In fact, he had not kept a close eye on anyone for this purpose. He was focusing on the overall performance of the group and not on any specific person. For the past few days, he had been more interested in watching Chitrangada than his soldiers. But he didn't want her to know that.

"Yes, I have a few candidates in mind," he lied. "I am looking into it. You know it's a difficult choice."

"I really like your commitment to the kingdom of Manipur," she said, leaning back. It looked like she had nothing more to say.

He smiled at her and kept silent. He tried to construct a sentence to express his love for her.

"You wanted to talk to me about something?" Chitrangada reminded him, her eyes closed already.

Arjuna noticed this. He had to speak before she fell asleep. "I don't know how to say this but, I have another proposal in mind which will help both you and the kingdom. And it will solve all of your problems, this time, permanently."

Chitrangada wasn't excited but she wanted to listen. She opened her eyes.

Arjuna hesitated.

Chitrangada was losing valuable time. She was impatient to hear his proposal.

Arjuna took a deep breath. "Listen, I know it might sound strange, but it may be the only solution."

Chitrangada waited, he was testing her patience.

"I think you should get married," Arjuna blurted out.

Chitrangada burst into loud laughter. Arjuna was surprised. It was a serious matter, but he didn't interrupt her. He found her laughter endearing.

"That's what the whole city has been telling me over the last few years," she said. "What is new? You are one of the kings of Indraprastha. I expected more from you."

"Well, actually, I might have found a suitable partner for you," he said, but Chitrangada was still laughing, so she couldn't hear him.

"I'm sorry," she said, slowly recovering from her mirth.

"What exactly are you proposing?" she asked.

"I am proposing to you," he said bluntly.

Chitrangada was silent. She just sat there, staring at him.

"I know this must be hard to process for you," he said. "We haven't spent a lot of time with each other and we don't know each other well, but I think we can work this out together." He could see Chitrangada getting nervous now. It was no easy decision to make. She would have to think long and hard before making a choice.

Chitrangada was not in love with anyone nor had her father found a suitable match for her. If she married Arjuna, it would surely solve the Manipuri crisis, but marriage was the most important question of her life. Did she love him with all her heart? Could she accept him as her husband and partner? The solution Arjuna had provided was not an impossible one. He was a royal himself, an excellent warrior and more importantly, marrying him would help her provide the kingdom with an heir. These were all good points, but there were some negatives as well. What if Arjuna left after sometime? Chitrangada wasn't ready to leave her land nor would she let her future son go with Arjuna to Indraprastha.

Arjuna waited for her to speak. Ulupi had not been a consideration for him in his decision-making process. He had no plans of meeting her again. Chitrangada was confused. She needed time to think and to consult her father and elders. Arjuna was ready to wait. But he realised they couldn't be friends anymore. Either they would get married or they would never talk to each other again.

"Let's talk to my father about it today evening," Chitrangada said.

Arjuna understood that there were some technical difficulties with their marriage. Also, he knew she wasn't in love with him, but at least she had not rejected him outright. That was a silver lining.

After she left, Arjuna did have second thoughts. He couldn't believe that he had not even thought about his two wives before taking this decision. It was almost like he had forgotten that they existed. How easily he had done away with them! He felt guilty about it, but what could he do? He had fallen in love with this woman and he was totally helpless to fight that feeling. He had to marry her or else live in pain for the rest of his life.

27

A Marriage is Finalised

Arjuna wondered why he was so desperate to marry Chitrangada. His journey was meant to be a lone one with minimal interaction with the outside world. When he started out on his pilgrimage, he had never considered the possibility of falling in love, and that too twice! But such is the power of love. A person in love is unstoppable. He is not afraid to try, he is never afraid to fail and he is ready to go to great lengths to reach his goal.

The meeting at the palace was held in the private resting room of King Chitravahana. Only the King, the Princess and Arjuna were present. Arjuna and Chitrangada sat next to each other, King Chitravahana in front of them.

"Arjuna, my daughter has told me that you have shown interest in marrying her," the King said. "Is this true?

"Yes, I would like to marry her. This marriage will not only give you a son-in-law but also an heir to the throne," Arjuna replied.

"I know that this marriage has numerous advantages. It can solve all of our problems but what my real concern is—what happens after that? Marriage isn't some sort of business deal. It is a ceremony bonding two people and assuring they spend the rest of their lives together. I need to be absolutely sure that I am giving my daughter's hand to someone who not only loves her but also respects her and will treat her well. Are you willing to promise me this?"

"Yes, I will do my best to treat her well. You have my word," Arjuna said immediately. There was no room for hesitation. Any delay would cause doubts in the King's mind.

"I trust you on this," the King smiled at him. "But there are a few things we should discuss before going forward."

Arjuna was all ears.

"My main concern is that you are not a member of the Kingdom of Manipur," the King said. "It's not a problem right now, but what if it creates problems after the marriage? I expect you may leave and continue on your journey. And my daughter, being your wife, will be bound by duty to travel with you. Even your future children will have to leave with you. The marriage will provide our kingdom with an heir but it is certain that you are going to leave Manipur and return to Indraprastha. What about that?"

"They don't have to come with me, they can stay here," Arjuna promised. He was eager to convince the King that the marriage was an excellent prospect.

Chitrangada was quiet. It was hard to tell what she was thinking.

The King spoke after a considered pause. "Well…once you provide us with an heir you can go back to Indraprastha when you want and return whenever you wish to do so. But the one tradition we cannot compromise on is that Chitrangada and her son cannot leave with you. They will stay here and look after the kingdom."

Arjuna confirmed this again. He was not against this arrangement at all.

"What about you, Chitrangada? If you have any problem with it, we can change our plans," he said, looking at her intently.

Chitrangada nodded her head. "It seems reasonable. Works well for the both of us." She turned to her father and requested him to arrange the marriage. She was happy to accept Arjuna as her husband.

Arjuna was pleased. But he did wonder if Chitrangada was forcing herself to get married for the sake of her kingdom. If she didn't like him, he would not disturb her after their marriage. But he was confident his charms would work on her.

King Chitravahana organised a huge ceremony on the palace grounds a week later. According to the Manipuri tradition, the whole process had to get over in one day. A holiday for the whole kingdom was declared. It was one of the most-awaited events in their history. Everyone wanted Chitrangada to get married and people loved Arjuna for offering to marry their Princess. It was a day of joy and celebration for the people of Manipur.

Arjuna had fallen in love for the third time. There was very little interaction between the Princess and him after the marriage was fixed because according to tradition, the bride and groom could not meet each other before the wedding. It was a week of waiting. He wanted to meet her but he had to be careful with Chitrangada. She was a disciplined person who followed the rules.

Both of them continued with their training. Arjuna noticed her training every day as usual. Any other princess would be busy with wedding preparations, involving herself with clothes and ornaments and the like. This made

Arjuna wonder again whether Chitrangada was really interested in marrying him. But he comforted himself with the knowledge that she was a committed, disciplined warrior who hated to miss her training sessions.

28

The Ceremony

On the day of the marriage Arjuna was gifted a set of clothes by the King. He wore a beautiful green, golden, patterned dhoti. Two gold-coated angavastrams hung from both his shoulders and were pinned together at the centre of his chest. The main attraction was his big, bright orange turban with a huge, green emerald at the front. There was a gold chain wound around the turban to give it a royal look.

The palace grounds, the venue, were packed. The whole of Manipur had arrived. There was no space to take a step. It was impossible to control the crowd. The army was there to manage the rush and the soldiers pushed aside people to make room for Arjuna to pass. They had a tough time. It was peak summer and the sun shone bright. Arjuna was already sweating heavily, he couldn't imagine how the crowd would survive the heat with so many sweaty bodies rubbing and pushing against each other. He understood they were ready to suffer that inconvenience for the sake of their beloved Princess. Her wedding was a dream come true for the whole kingdom.

Arjuna was escorted by the army to the stage at the centre of the grounds. The crowd was going wild with joy. People wanted to touch him as he walked past them. Arjuna saw the joy he was bringing to them. He was about to remove a huge burden form their shoulders and secure their future. They could live happily now knowing that their children could dream of a bright future. The stage was a huge square with the four corners marked with strong pillars. Green plants and creepers covered the pillars. From the four pillars, ropes were drawn, connecting all the four points. From these ropes hung the main attraction: hundreds of bright-coloured tulips.

King Chitravahana loved maintaining his gardens and he had all kinds of flowers and plants in them. In fact, he had completed a short course in botany recently and also written a book on his personal experience about growing the royal gardens. The flowers used at the venue were special hybrids. There were pink, purple, blue, green and white tulips to dazzle the crowd. There were of all sizes and shapes and tastefully arranged on the stage. A true visual treat for all the guests!

The Pandit, dressed in a white dhoti and angavastram, stood on the stage, chanting the marriage mantras. He had a huge, protruding belly and his dhoti was pushed down below his waist to accommodate it. His head was shaved except for a small tuft at the back. He had hàir all over his chest, his belly, his back and shoulders.

King Chitravahana walked up to Arjuna. "Thank you for marrying my daughter," he said, and hugged his son-in-law.

"Thank you for letting me marry your daughter," Arjuna replied.

They waited for Chitrangada to arrive. There was a huge roar from the crowd when she came. Arjuna was stunned.

Chitrangada didn't look this way when he last saw her training. She had turned into a gracious, beautiful princess, the epitome of charm. There was no limit to Arjuna's happiness. He was lucky to have found her. Draupadi and Ulupi were already his, and now Chitrangada too. He was a great warrior, a Pandava, Prince of Indraprastha, but there were many men better than him in every way in the world. He didn't know the secret of his success. Maybe he was destined to be with beautiful women.

Chitrangada wore a light pink blouse which fit her perfectly. For the first time, Arjuna noticed her full breasts and her deep cleavage. The sleeveless blouse was a masterpiece, designed by the finest designers. It was dotted with diamonds which reflected the bright sunlight. Chitrangada's dhoti was two layered. The deeper layer was a light pink plain one which looked like it was made from the finest cloth on earth. Over that she wore a semi-transparent layer with a flowery pattern. It was an excellent combination. A thin cloth covered her head.

Her accessories were many and glamorous; she wore huge triangular earrings made of pink emeralds. At the centre of her forehead was a big, round, red bindi. She had also got her nose pierced for the occasion. The nose ring was a huge diamond with a small gold chain hanging from it. Even though it was too big for her face, it gave her a royal look. She had a perfect, taut abdomen since she was a trained warrior. She was a little muscular for a princess, her arms showed clear-cut, small biceps.

Arjuna admired her perfect figure during the marriage ceremony. Once the wedding was sermonised, the newly-wed Arjuna was escorted, with great fanfare, to spend his first night with his wife at the palace. King Chitravahana had done his best to give the room a romantic touch. Arjuna couldn't wait to get close to his beautiful bride, but he had to wait for her approval. He knew that even if she didn't love him, she would definitely want a child from him for the sake of her kingdom's future.

Arjuna mustered some confidence and walked up to her. As he walked, he noticed a stand at the centre of the room on which a medium-sized bowl was kept. It had a number of small, beautiful floating flowers in it. They made the room smell like heaven. Both husband and wife had bathed and changed into a fresh set of clothes as was the custom. So, Arjuna was back to his light, white, cotton dhoti. Chitrangada was just wearing a single cloth, tied around her waist and then pulled up at both ends to cover her breasts. The two ends were tied from behind at the nape of her neck. Her hair was tied into a bun at the top of her head.

"I know it's hard for you," Arjuna said gently. "You forced this marriage on yourself for the kingdom and for your people. But I did this, you know...for...love."

Chitrangada looked at him, surprised that he had confessed his love. She didn't feel angry at all. She stood up and went closer to him. Her face was bare, without any makeup, but her skin was glowing. She looked perfect in Arjuna's eyes.

"Well, thank you for your confession," she said. "I've always known that you like me." Her tone was tender and playful.

Arjuna was lost for words. This was the first time he had confessed his feelings to a woman.

"I have seen many strong warriors, princes, men just like you," she continued. "But I find you special. I have started developing deep feelings for you. I love the fact that you are trying to help stabilise our kingdom during difficult times and I am very grateful for that."

Arjuna smiled. Her words made him very happy.

"To be honest, I am a little nervous," she said. After a few seconds of silence, she continued. "I have never fallen in love before, never felt a love like this before."

He understood why she was having a problem dealing with it. She was a focused warrior who had dedicated her entire life to her kingdom. She hadn't thought of anything else, or enjoyed life like other princesses would. She hadn't experienced the pleasure of being with a lover before or even thought about it. Her lack of experience made her nervous about marriage. She was scared that she wouldn't be good at expressing her love.

"It's all going to be fine," he soothed her. "I love you just the way you are, don't change for my sake. I know that over time you will get comfortable with our new life. You are one of the most amazing people I have ever met. You should be proud of everything you've done for your kingdom."

She gave him a smile in return.

Arjuna hugged her, hoping it would not make her uncomfortable. There was no rush. They had all the time in the world to get comfortable with each other.

29

Life after Marriage

The next morning, Arjuna woke up late. Chitrangada had left for her training. Arjuna looked around the room and went back to sleep. The night had been exciting and exhausting. He didn't know from where she had got the energy to get up early. As the days passed, the two of them became more and more comfortable with each other. Chitrangada was a silent soul, but she was happy to be around Arjuna. She didn't put her happiness into words though Arjuna could sense it.

One day, Arjuna was training some children since he enjoyed spending time with them. Chitrangada had come to watch. The children were below ten years of age. They wore mini dhotis and ran around, some swinging small swords or sticks in the air. Arjuna tried to give them some instructions but they were too restless to listen to him. He could control great warriors, but these children were impossible to train.

"Tough task though, managing these little warriors," Chitrangada laughed, watching them play.

Arjuna shook his head. "That's the beauty of them, isn't it?" He was happy to see Chitrangada so relaxed and comfortable around him. They were a real couple now, enjoying their togetherness.

Arjuna watched her walk over to the children. He had heard many stories about how much she loved children and how many orphans she had taken under her wing. A five year old, lost in his own imaginary world, swinging his sword at some big monster flying over him, attracted Chitrangada's attention. He wore a small dhoti loosely tied at his waist. His head was shaven and he had a round face and a small belly. Chitrangada kneeled down next to him. He stopped swinging his sword and looked alarmed. But after a few seconds, he recognised her and smiled at her. It turned out that all these boys had lost their parents and Chitrangada was looking after them.

She pointed at the boy with her index finger and acted as if she wanted to fight. Her finger was her sword. The young boy was back to fighting mode; he raised his sword and screamed. Chitrangada used her finger as her sword and the child swung his small sword around. After a few swings, Chitrangada dodged his sword and tickled him. The boy started laughing and wriggling around. She tickled his small belly. She was happy to make him laugh. After a few seconds, she gave him a hug, lifted him up and kissed his cheeks twice. Arjuna for once wanted to be in that little boy's position.

Then, she called out to the other boys, holding the boy in her arms. It seemed like he was her favourite. The other boys came running to hug her. They all loved her and she loved them back with equal fervour. Arjuna realised that his wife wasn't as serious and focused as she looked. He was delighted to see her reveal more of her real self freely. He felt they were ready to have a child together. The time was right for it.

30

Leaving Once Again

Arjuna had spent four months in Manipur, the longest he had stayed put during his journey. He only had a couple of months left to go back to Indraprastha. One day, King Chitravahana, Chitrangada and Arjuna were sitting in the King's chambers. Arjuna had to bring up the topic of his departure. It was no easy subject to broach.

"Arjuna, how is the training going? Are the soldiers doing well?" King Chitravahana asked.

"Yes, they are," Arjuna said. "I love the training sessions, but it seems like the soldiers don't need me anymore. They are in perfect form now. All I have been doing is guiding them through the mental aspects of it."

"Our army has always been the best and our former General, bless him, did a fine job with them."

"Yes"

"And have you made any progress in choosing a new General?"

"Well, I might have found the one. And I think this decision should have been taken a long time ago," Arjuna replied.

Chitrangada closed the book she was reading and looked at Arjuna.

"Well, who is it? Better late than never," the King said.

"She will lead the army like no man has ever done before. She will make Manipur great again," Arjuna said, looking at Chitrangada.

The choice was easy, the minute he saw Chitrangada fight; he had decided she was it. She was the most dedicated soldier he had ever seen. King Chitravahana understood what he was implying. But he wasn't sure if he wanted his daughter to lead the army. He didn't want her to take on this time-consuming job. She had just got married and he wanted his daughter to have a personal life.

"We all know Chitrangada is the right choice to lead the army, the perfect choice. I suggest you and the cabinet atleast consider it," Arjuna insisted.

King Chitravahana checked on his daughter. She neither objected nor showed any signs of delight.

"Arjuna, she is a good choice," the King said, taking a breath before revealing a secret. "It may be difficult now that she is about to become a mother."

Arjuna was stunned, delighted and disoriented. Chitrangada was pregnant? He had been waiting for this moment forever.

Chitranagdha was expecting her first child. She had just found out and informed only her father about it.

"This is the best day of my life. Thank you, thank you very much," Arjuna ran to his wife and embraced her. He was about to become a father. What greater joy could one ask for?

Chitrangada too shed tears of joy. She thanked Arjuna many times.

King Chitravahana was overjoyed at his daughter's happiness. "Arjuna, I am forever grateful to you," he said.

"You have given us everything. We the people of Manipur are indebted to you."

"I am forever indebted to you for giving me a wonderful wife and child," Arjuna said.

The three of them savoured the good news for a while. Arjuna and Chitrangada held each other and whispered endearments in soft tones.

In a while, Arjuna spoke to the King about the army once more. He was confident Chitrangada could take charge once she delivered their child. During her pregnancy she would find it tough to do her routine training and oversee the soldiers. Once the child was born, she could get back to it. The men could handle themselves for a little while on their own. King Chitravahana wanted to find a solution to this question quickly.

"She seems to be the right fit but is there any other choice we can consider?" he asked calmly.

"I know you don't want your daughter to go on the field and train with the soldiers every day, but let us ask her about it," Arjuna said.

They looked at her. She saw her father was nervous. She needed to instill some confidence in him. "Father, I know you love me and you don't want me to risk my life anymore, but that's what warriors are trained to do," she said. "I know I will have a child with me soon. But, the soldiers, I have trained and fought with them my whole life. I know them better than anyone else. I can perform the duty to the fullest. Just give me a chance. I want my child to be proud of me."

King Chitravahana was much moved. Her request was accepted. "I think you make a fair point, both of you. I will appoint her as the next General of the Manipuri army. The cabinet will have no objections to this," he promised.

Arjuna hugged his wife again. He had only two more months of exile left.

"Will you be leaving us soon?" the King asked.

"It is difficult for me to part from my wife and child," Arjuna said. "But I hope to see more of your country before the end of my exile."

He noticed Chitrangada had started to look very sad. But he knew she was a strong woman, and unlike Draupadi and Ulupi, she wouldn't keep thinking about him after he was gone. She would recover sooner than them.

"I know I can't force you to stay," the King said with a sigh. "I hope you will come back as soon as possible. My daughter and your child will be waiting for you."

King Chitravahana began to weep. Arjuna went across the hall and hugged his old friend. The King left the room in a few minutes. Arjuna walked up to Chitrangada. She was teary eyed. This broke his heart. He didn't want to see her cry. It was terrible to see a brave and beautiful warrior like her dissolving into tears. He felt her pain deeply. She had found someone to love after a lifetime of loneliness and now he was leaving her side.

"I will come back," he comforted her. "Our child will enter this world in a few months."

Chitrangada nodded but didn't reply. Tears were still flowing down her cheeks.

Arjuna held her face in his hands. "I hope our child becomes just like you, strong, brave, passionate, loving and most important, a beautiful person. You are an independent woman...you don't need me or anyone else to support you. Promise me that you won't keep thinking about me after I leave. Promise me that you will perform your duties like you always have. Promise me you will make our child the greatest warrior in the world."

She nodded.

"I will love you and remember you, always," he said as he hugged her.

It would be much more difficult than anticipated for Chitrangada to do her duties after he left. She loved him more than she knew.

* * *

Finally, the day for Arjuna to depart dawned. King Chitravahana had arranged a grand farewell for him. King Chitravahana had also arranged for horses and a charioteer to take him to any location he wanted. The palace grounds were full again. The crowd had come to bid goodbye to their Prince.

Thank you, son" the King said. "Have a safe journey ahead and hope you find whatever you are seeking."

Arjuna touched Chitravahana's feet and asked him for his blessing. Arjuna's chariot awaited him. He saw the crowd waving at him and waved back before stepping into his chariot. Arjuna looked at Chitrangada from a distance, she smiled at him proudly. She would not weep in public.

Subhadra

31

Arjuna on the Move

Arjuna ditched his chariot at the border of Manipur and decided to walk again. He had a couple more months left on his journey and wanted to make the most of it. The thought of going back to Indraprastha consumed him most of the time. He kept thinking about his brothers and how they must have spent the past year. Yudhishthira's time with Draupadi had just ended, and now, Bhim would have the pleasure for a year and then, it would be Arjuna's turn.

The journey had taught him more than he had anticipated—less of a philosophical and more of a romantic journey. He had married two beautiful women, a Naga Princess and the Princess of Manipur in ten short months. Along with that, he had learnt to survive in the wild, eat whatever food was available and share it with others in a loving manner. He had seen how the villagers valued food and understood its importance. He was no longer an arrogant prince, blind to the suffering of the less fortunate.

Arjuna travelled throughout the north. Luckily, he found a loyal companion along the way. It was a wild, but very friendly dog. There were a few wounds on its dark brown body from the fights with the other forest dogs. This wild dog followed Arjuna around as he walked on.

The dog reminded him of the small boy, Regi, and his more domesticated pet. Arjuna had not liked dogs before the trip, but his close encounters with the two dogs had converted him to a dog lover. Now he knew why people considered a dog man's best friend. He felt homesick sometimes and he wondered how big Bhim must have grown. Bhim always set high standards when it came to body building. He was one of the pioneers of body building. The previous year, Bhim had grown almost double in terms of his weight and muscles. He worked out regularly and ate well. He was always seen at the training grounds, lifting heavy logs.

Nakul and Sahadev were the ones he missed the most. They were the youngest and his favourites. He spent the most time with these two among his brothers. Yudhishthira was all about management and Bhim mostly related to training, but with Nakul and Sahadev he could talk about many interesting topics. The topics ranged from women to fitness to personal grooming. They talked to Arjuna about their love lives. They asked him to teach them techniques to impress the girls they liked. Sometimes, when they fought about things, Arjuna used to help them make up. He was both a friend and an elder brother. He was dying to see them.

Draupadi was a distant memory now. Even though he was thinking about her, he didn't miss her too much. He knew his brother wouldn't let her feel sad for one moment. And besides, Arjuna had met Ulupi, and he had Chitrangada to share his love with now.

* * *

Arjuna arrived at the Sapth Sindhu region along the Indus River in time. He needed to find a good place to spend the next couple of months. He was still interested in meeting beautiful women and he remembered an old friend had spoken about a very attractive lady who lived in Dwaraka, which was not far off. This was back when Arjuna was temporarily residing at Drona's ashram; back when the Kauravas were on good terms with the Pandavas. There, Arjuna met Gaddi, a member of the Yadav clan and became friends with him. This man had given him some information about a beautiful girl called Subhadra. Her skin was as white as milk and she wore simple clothing. Her grace and charm were legendary.

Arjuna wasn't a teenager anymore but his interest in women persisted. He decided to go to Dwaraka and meet Subhadra. Women opened up new worlds for him and he would always be grateful for their presence in his life. But there were difficulties in his path. People would recognise him easily in Dwaraka because he had a very close association with that kingdom back when the Pandavas and Kauravas were together. Now Dwaraka was a Kaurava-friendly commune. Another problem—Subhadra was Krishna's sister. Not a bad thing, but a hindrance. Krishna frequented Dwaraka to meet his sister and brother. So, the best option for Arjuna would be to go in disguise and the best disguise he could pull off with ease was that of a hermit.

His hair was long, he hadn't washed it for weeks and it was all rough and dry and untidily tied into a bun at the top of head. His beard had grown since the time he shaved for his wedding to Chitrangada. He used a white cloth which he had got as a gift from Manipur to fashion a hermit's costume. Hermits had to look rough and untidy because they didn't really care about the world. They spent their time meditating and lived along the banks of rivers or on the mountains. Arjuna was determined to play the part. He donned the disguise and set out for Dwaraka in search of Subhadra.

32

Dwaraka, the Golden City

Dwaraka city was totally under the control of Krishna's brother, Balarama. Dwaraka was planned and constructed in a radial pattern; the palace and the important buildings were all located at the centre, at the outskirts lived people with low incomes who couldn't afford the expensive lifestyle of the centre. The city was also called the "golden city" since most of the buildings were made of gold or gold-plated.

Dwaraka was a luxurious city. The taxes were high but the privileges were many for those who could afford the taxes. The rich stayed at the centre and enjoyed the many facilities like free transport. But Balarama didn't force the poor to pay heavy taxes, they paid as much as they could and were given the basic necessities to live a life. Arjuna roamed around the city, trying to understand his new surroundings. He was figuring out a way to reach Subhadra. The only way he could do it was through Balarama. She rarely made any public appearances and stayed in her palace. Her brother Balarama was very protective of her and restricted her movements.

Arjuna had to find a way. He noticed that he was getting a lot of attention from people as he walked along. They greeted him with folded hands, they didn't try to stop him or talk to him. It was as if he was being worshipped like God. The people of Dwaraka were known to be great devotees of Lord Shiva and they worshipped everything and anything connected to the Lord. They paid special homage to hermits who meditated for years praying to Lord Shiva.

Arjuna decided to take advantage of this. If the people were so religious, their King Balarama too would be as devout. If he wanted Balarama's attention, a temple would be the best place to target. The only temple in Dwaraka was situated at the outskirts and not at the centre. It was almost 200 years old and had stood there even before the city was built. So Balarama didn't demolish it, he just remade it.

This happened to be the biggest Shiva temple in the whole of the Sindhu region and also the most visited. Every year, people came here to offer prayers, money and food to the Lord. It was under Balarama's control and he did a very good job of overseeing it. He spent a huge part of the taxes he collected on the temple's upkeep. People didn't mind this, though some of the money could have been used for developing the city. Since the money went to Lord Shiva, no one objected to Balarama's decision.

Balarama visited the temple every day at sunrise to seek the blessings of Lord Shiva before starting his day. Arjuna could easily position himself there and try to catch his attention. He scanned the temple carefully. It was not that impressive in terms of its architecture but it was a very expensive affair. The whole temple was gold-plated. Only the floors were white marble. The temple was built in the shape of a square with a huge golden dome on top, one of the additions made by Balarama. There was no entrance door. The place of worship was open to all of Dwaraka.

A series of stairs lead to the temple since it stood at a height. Arjuna went inside and he noticed that an idol of

Lord Shiva was kept inside a small room. There was a huge queue of people to see the idol, beautifully decorated with the finest cloth and jewels. The eyes were diamonds, the rest covered with gold and emeralds. Arjuna saw people standing in line holding offerings like milk and rice. The rich devotees had a special line with offerings of precious jewelry.

There was a large pond at the back of the temple. Arjuna stood next to it, looking out for a place where he could sit and meditate (or act like he was). He spotted a huge banyan tree beside a huge stone statue of Lord Shiva. In it, Shiva stood on one leg, the other flexed horizontally to his thigh. His red tongue stuck out, his eyes including the third eye were wide open. He held a trishul with both hands.

Arjuna made himself comfortable under the huge canopy of the banyan tree; the leaves gave him excellent shade. The place was perfect. Many people came there to see the statue and it was also a comfortable spot. He could sit there and watch people all day. And he did exactly that. He sat in a meditating posture with his legs folded over each other, his hands on his knees. He closed his eyes when someone came close to him, but made sure he didn't leave the spot the whole day, till the temple closed.

The next day, he repeated the same routine. And it happened that he actually managed to meditate the whole morning. He concentrated on his breathing and found it very helpful after he was done. The trouble was that he wasn't able to attract attention by doing any of this. He had to try harder to get noticed by Balarama. He understood that he needed to do something which would attract people to him. He decided to offer them free food. He had a big stock of fruits that he had brought from Manipur. So, the next day he got the fruits to the temple.

33

One Step Closer to Subhadra

Arjuna didn't just sit around the whole day. He offered fruits to all the poor people who lived around the temple. He wanted to attract attention, so he focused on the helpless ones. In the afternoons, he went back to the shade of his banyan tree. Soon, he got results. His plan was finally working. First, he had just a few people coming in, but then his audience grew as rich people also started following him. Rumours had started to spread that he was one of the oldest devotees of Lord Shiva. So, people flocked around him, meditated along with him, and the rich started offering food to the poor just like him. In a couple of weeks, they started served mid-day meals to anyone who was hungry.

Arjuna brought in enough people to fill the space outside the temple. He was the most popular person in Dwaraka and the banyan tree was the most happening place. Every day the number of visitors increased dramatically and this also helped the temple earn high revenues. This was enough to bring him to Balarama's notice. Arjuna had pulled off the victory he desired and also managed to persuade the wealthy people in town to feed the needy. He was proud of himself even if he was just pretending to be a monk.

34

Meeting Balarama

Finally the day came. It was late evening and the temple was about to close. Arjuna was sitting there, surrounded by a couple of devotees. He wanted them to leave so that he could relax. He saw two horsemen riding towards him. They wore gold-plated armour and he was sure they were Balarama's men. They halted a few metres away.

One of the soldiers stepped in front of Arjuna, his hands still folded. He had a devotee's smile on his face. "Om Nama Shivaya," he said.

The other soldier repeated the chant.

"Om Nama Shivaya," Arjuna said softly.

The soldier spoke nervously. "Swamiji, we are delighted to have you in Dwaraka. The people of Dwaraka are lucky to have a guru like you in our city's temple."

Arjuna smiled. He didn't want to act too serious or very friendly.

The other soldier added, "Swamiji, our King Balarama is very pleased with your presence. You have helped the people become more religious, they are visiting the temple more often. The King is really happy about it and he would like to offer you something in return."

Arjuna was pleased by the soldier's manner. He was very respectful and was almost kneeling down in front of Arjuna. For a moment Arjuna thought of quitting his old life and becoming a hermit/godman. The benefits were endless, the work, easy. He didn't have to do anything and he got so much respect and attention from people. Even food and housing were no problem at all for him. Arjuna didn't give a reply to the soldiers for a while. He didn't want to jump into it too soon.

"Swamiji, the King wants to thank you for your blessings, just give you a token of his gratitude. He won't take much of your time," the soldier assured him.

"Son, I would love to meet your King but we hermits don't take anything in return for the services we offer," Arjuna said.

The soldiers quickly stood up, rushed towards their horses and desperately started attaching the chariot to the horses to make the arrangements for Arjuna's journey. When it comes to God and hermits, people will go to any length to please them.

When Arjuna sat in the chariot, the soldiers tried their best to make him comfortable. They offered to hold an umbrella over his head to shade him from the sun.

"I'm fine," Arjuna said, telling them not to worry.

The soldiers smiled at him respectfully and they headed out to meet Balarama. Arjuna was taken not to the palace as he expected, but to a guesthouse at the edge of the city. He was escorted inside by the soldiers.

Balarama welcomed him with a smile and folded hands. "Om Nama Shivaya. Welcome Swamiji," he said, bending down to Arjuna's knees. He seemed very excited about the hermit's arrival.

Arjuna smiled at him. He had decided that he wouldn't speak much to Balarama because hermits don't talk much.

"We are honoured to have such a great man visit Dwaraka," Balarama beamed at him.

The main hall of the house was huge and airy. There was a central courtyard, where there was a small garden. There was no roof over that area and the evening light fell on it. The house was simple, neat and minimally furnished. It wasn't very extravagant and expensive but it was beautiful in its simplicity.

Arjuna was escorted to a chair by the soldiers and Balarama. He was lavished with attention and care. Arjuna refused to sit down because it would go against his lifestyle principles. Balarama agreed to it and offered him a floor mat. Balarama and the two soldiers sat on the floor in front of Arjuna. Their hands were folded in prayer.

"Swamiji," Balarama leaned forward to make himself more audible. "Swamiji, I don't want to bother you for long but we in Dwaraka rarely get a chance to meet a spiritual person like you. Swamiji, we all believe in Lord Shiva, he is our only protector and destroyer. Swamiji, we are grateful for your presence among us. It feels like we are getting a glimpse of the Lord himself. So, I wanted to take this opportunity to thank you."

Arjuna had a smile on his face. He didn't want to show any of his emotions or make a mistake by mentioning Subhadra.

"Swamiji, and the great work you have started at the Shiva temple, the people of Dwaraka are very grateful for that," Balarama said.

Arjuna smiled. There was more praise on the way.

"Swamiji, Dwaraka had been facing a lot of inequality issues recently. The rich here only care about their money and fortune, they never tried helping the poor, and maybe I didn't devote myself enough to help the less fortunate. But your efforts and success have helped me learnt a lot. I can see that that the people are now trying to help each other. They have realised that it is only by helping each other that we can attain happiness. I humbly thank you on behalf of all of Dwaraka for this selfless service. You have changed the way we think about life."

Arjuna realised that Balarama wasn't a bad person as he had thought. Yes, he did lean towards the rich and the powerful, but he was willing to learn.

"Swamiji, I don't know for how long you here in Dwaraka, but it's my request that you stay here at our guesthouse for the rest of your stay. And we beg you to live here or a few more weeks and shower us with your blessings," Balarama said. "I would also greatly appreciate it if you gave my sister spiritual lessons while you are here."

Arjuna thought about it for a minute, then, agreed. He didn't want to seem too eager to meet Subhadra. "Yes, maybe it will be a good experience for all. I can extend my stay for a few days," he said.

"Thank you, Swamiji, thank you," Balarama was overwhelmed with gratitude.

Balarama had one more request but he hesitated before speaking. He didn't want to burden the great hermit and make him leave Dwaraka. He had already asked for a lot.

"Swamiji, my sister Subhadra," Balarama said, and Arjuna's face lit up on hearing her name.

Arjuna sensed an opportunity. He jumped in, "Child, don't worry, you may place you request freely. There is no need to be nervous."

Balarama nodded and continued, "My sister is getting married very soon, so, I want her to be on her best behaviour, be sensible, spiritual and focused like you when she goes to her husband's place. I want her to be a better person. It would be wonderful if you teach her some values and principles that would help her in the future." Balarama folded his hands in prayer and closed his eyes as he placed his request.

For Arjuna, first of all it was a shocker to hear that Subhadra was getting married, but the good news was that if he accepted the offer he could spend a lot of time with her. He would impress her in a short time. Of that he was sure.

Arjuna had a smile on his face when he said, "I will do my best to teach your sister all the principles I have learnt over the past two decades. Om Nama Shivaya, may Lord Shiva bless your sister."

Balarama was really happy about it. He loved his sister more than anything in the world and he was delighted that the hermit would give her lessons. He asked Arjuna if he needed any special arrangements to be made for Arjuna's stay.

"No, nothing at all," Arjuna said.

Arjuna assured him that he had no special needs. The three of them left the room with folded hands and bowed heads, careful not to turns their backs on the hermit since it was a sign of disrespect. One of the soldiers stumbled on a chair as he walked, but he went on. Arjuna had to control his laughter. He didn't expect Balarama, elder brother of the great Lord Krishna, to be fooled so easily.

Arjuna walked around the house after they left. The house was cool and comfortable because the roof made of tiles which warded off the heat and the stone-flooring.

It was very quiet and peaceful inside. Arjuna noticed a single house nearby, but there was no other building to be seen in the vicinity. He sat down on a cozy chair and thought about Subhadra. Who was she getting married to? Balarama had not mentioned his name. It was no easy task that he was planning to take on. Maybe the best method for him to impress her would be to convert her to a hermit like himself and make her break the marriage, but he had very little time to do that. He thought and thought, and drifted off to sleep in the chair itself. He slept undisturbed the whole night.

35

Finally, Subhadra

The next morning, Arjuna woke up late.

"Swamiji, Swamiji," he heard a woman's voice.

Arjuna took some time to shake off his sleep. He extricated himself from the chair and stood up on wobbly legs. His vision got more focused and he saw that a short, old lady was standing in front of him.

"Swamiji," she said, waiting for Arjuna to stand up straight. He was trying to maintain his balance, still recovering from his sleep.

"Swamiji, Subhadra Devi is waiting outside, she seeks your permission to meet you," the lady said.

Subhadra's name quickly alerted him. All this while he had longed to meet her, and now that she was there, he wasn't ready and at his best. He had just woken up. He needed to comb his hair and spruce up his clothes.

"Swami, Subhadra Devi is keen on meeting you," the old lady was persistent. She repeated herself, suspecting he hadn't heard her. She was Subhadra's loyal and longtime helper/guardian Padma, and she made sure her mistress got what she wanted. She wasn't going to leave unless Arjuna agreed to the request.

Arjuna nodded.

Padma set off to call Subhadra.

Arjuna tried his best to make himself presentable in the few minutes he had. He adjusted his dhoti which had loosened up and was almost falling from his waist. Other than that, there was nothing he could do to improve his appearance.

Subhadra entered the room.

Arjuna had just finished tightening his dhoti. He was still holding the dhoti with one hand when he saw her. His dream woman...the one he had longed to meet for so long.

Subhadra had a similar dress sense to Ulupi when it came to the amount of clothing (very little) she wore, but she was a little more regal in appearance. She wore a dark purple blouse, transiently shaded darker on the lower part. Sensuously fitting around her breasts. A beautiful sight indeed! She wore a huge, white angavastram that covered her abdomen and a light blue dhoti. Even with the angavastram, her sensuous curves were still visible. She pulled it across her body, trying to cover more skin, conscious about being in the presence of a hermit. All his wives were beautiful, but Arjuna found her flawless.

"Namaste, Swamiji," Subhadra said as she bowed down and folded her hands before Arjuna. She had such a sweet voice and a sweeter smile on her lips. She revealed a little of her cleavage as she bent down, but pulled her angavastram across her body quickly.

This made Arjuna understand how difficult it was to become a hermit and renounce human pleasures and live in total isolation. Maybe Arjuna himself could control all the other desires like hunger or love of money, but it was impossible to not desire beauties like Subhadra, Ulupi,

Draupadi and Chitrangada. He could never be an actual hermit and of this he was sure. He had set out for a year's pilgrimage and ended up marrying two women, she would be his third.

"Om Nama Shivaya," she said as she raised her head. The sun was just rising and the rays hit her face directly.

Subhadra had applied light but elegant makeup. She had a thin, black line on her eyelids to highlight her eyes. Her eyebrows were shapely and long. Her nose was pierced but she wore no ring. She had big, round, eyes. Her cheekbones were prominent, and her milky white skin was glowing. Her short hair was pulled back tightly and tied up into a ponytail.

"Swamiji, Om Nama…" she repeated.

"Om Nama Shivaya," he said finally.

She smiled at that and came closer to him. "Swamji, I am really excited to learn from you," she said. "I want to understand life the way you have experienced it. I am really thankful for your help and will do my best to understand what you say."

Arjuna smiled at her. "I will try and teach you everything I know," he said. "I will make you a more experienced and better person. We are going to have a great time together." Arjuna stepped back; he had to maintain a certain distance from her. He asked her if there was a place where they could meditate. Somewhere quiet, a lawn or a garden, a spot in the lap of nature.

"Yes, Swamiji, our lawn outside the house is very peaceful and quiet. That would be a very good place for us," she said, excited.

"Very well then, let us go there," he said, wary of denying any of her requests. She was so innocent and beautiful. He had already decided that he would never hurt her and would try and be her mentor and teacher. Krishna had once said to him that women are attracted to wise older men. They felt safe and comfortable and well looked after in their company. Arjuna had seen a lot of young, beautiful women fall in love with men who were at least a decade or two older than them, not all of them kings. He was fifteen years older than Subhadra in his estimation. So, he still had a good chance of winning her over.

"Do go ahead and I will be there in a few minutes," he said.

"Yes, Swamiji," said an eager Subhadra as she hurried away.

Arjuna had to freshen up. He was not going out there to join her in this half-asleep and dishevelled state.

36

The First Session

Arjuna freshened up and made himself look presentable. Then, he went down to the lawn where Subhadra was waiting for him. She was stretching her legs, getting herself ready for the session. She sat down on the ground, extended her legs to the fullest and tried to touch her toes with their fingers. She alternated between both legs and seemed to manage easily. By the looks of it she was very flexible and in good shape. But the one thing Arjuna didn't understand was why she was stretching, it was meant to be plain meditation. Maybe she was expecting yoga classes from him. Not that he was averse to it. He would enjoy teaching her yoga and watching her do it. He decided to add yoga to the list of things which he would teach her and learn with her.

"Namaste, Swamiji, I was just warming up," she said, breathing deeply. "Trying to loosen my muscles and joints. They can get pretty stiff in the mornings."

"Good. Very good," Arjuna said. She was right; one's joints do get a little stiff in the mornings. He always had joint problems when he used to be in training back in Indraprastha and stretching exercises were the worst part of his training days. But they were the most important too, so, he had to go through with them. Krishna, who was his personal trainer, had stressed heavily on his stretching. It was no surprise to him that Krishna's sister, Subhadra, loved stretching.

The lawn where they stood was a spacious one, paved with red bricks which had a matte finish. It was a rectangular space surrounded by huge trees which covered and protected the lawn from peering eyes. The compound wall running around the building was tall and made of polished, heavy stones. It was a perfectly secluded and suitable place for their sessions. Arjuna found a spot just a little away from the wall and sat down. Subhadra quickly followed him.

"Now, follow what I'm doing, close your eyes and take deep, long breaths," he said. "Very slowly, take a deep, long, breath. Try and take in as much air as your lungs can hold. And concentrate on the air while you are inhaling. Take it in." Arjuna demonstrated as he took a deep breath.

Subhadra copied him. She took a deep breath, her chest pumped up as she took the breath. The angavastram was pushed to the side as she inhaled. The sight of her abdomen and her breasts distracted Arjuna. He didn't know how he could conduct the session without staring at her. So, he tried closing his eyes but that lasted only for a few seconds.

"Deep breaths. Try and concentrate on your breathing." He kept repeating, talking more to himself than her. He didn't know what else to say. This was all he knew about meditation and spirituality. That was the only thing he remembered from his yoga training.

They continued in this way for a few minutes. Arjuna was just watching her do the breathing exercises. She closed her eyes and did them with great sincerity and he saw that she was enjoying the session. This was really very enlightening for him. Suddenly, Subhadra opened her eyes.

Arjuna was caught red-handed, but he immediately said, "Now open your eyes". That was quick thinking on his part. "How was it? Do you feel fresh, relaxed and clean from the inside?" he asked.

"Yes," she exhaled heavily again. "Yes, Swamiji, it was refreshing I need to do this every day."

"It's very good for your body and your soul. I would definitely recommend daily practice."

"Swamiji, I was wondering about how you managed to meditate for so many years without any food or water and survive the extreme climate of the mountains. It is really hard to concentrate there, isn't it?" She sounded very curious. Clearly she wasn't the type of person who was able to concentrate for long.

Arjuna smiled at her as if all those years of sacrifice were nothing for him. He could do much more.

"It is not easy to do it, but we are mentally prepared to sacrifice ourselves for the Lord," he said. "We pray and meditate till we see the Lord, till we are stopped by Him. Being a sanyasi and surviving the extreme climate with no food is not a miracle, it is pure will power and strength. The only thing which helped us survive those years was desire. The desire to get a glimpse of the Lord." He knew a little about hermits, he had met a few on his travels.

Subhadra was listening very carefully. She wanted to know more about their lifestyle.

"It is difficult but it is definitely worth it in the end," he paused. "You know, my story was a little different."

Subhadra sat with her chin resting on her hands, and legs folded. She was very interested to hear more.

He noticed how alert she was. He could not make any mistakes in his story, it had to flow smoothly.

"It wasn't my dream to go to the Himalayas and meditate, it wasn't my dream to be a sanyasi," he said. "In fact, I didn't have any intention of leaving my world and family for spiritual enlightenment."

"I was the prince of the largest kingdom in the country, yes, I was a prince before this," he said, watching Subhadra's eyes grow wide with wonder.

"A prince? I didn't expect that," she said.

"Yes, I know it will come as a big surprise, but I was a materialistic and greedy royal," he confessed. "I enjoyed money more than anyone else. I craved all the things money could buy and more. It was a good life back then but it was meaningless. People constantly strive to live that life but I have lived it, and it isn't very rewarding in the end." He found it easy to weave this tale. A prince giving up his kingdom to attain peace was not a tough story to cook up.

"Then what happened, Swamiji? What made you change your mind and leave all the riches and the power? You had everything anyone would ever want, didn't you?" she asked.

Arjuna exhaled deeply, it was tough for him to say why, since that would bring back some real memories. He was mixing up his real past with the story he had cooked up. But he went ahead anyway.

"It was this girl I fell in love with. She was the reason. Love can make you do things which are beyond your imagination." Arjuna was using the oldest trick in the book. Tragic love. But it was working on Subhadra.

"The girl, she was beautiful, and I had not spoken to her even once. But I loved her more than all the money and wealth on earth; I was ready to do anything for her. She was a princess, and I was sure I would get married to her alone... but I couldn't talk to her, I was too..." he paused.

"Afraid to lose her. You didn't want to lose her," Subhadra continued. She was deep in the heart of the story.

Arjuna was laughing on the inside, he didn't know why he was doing this to her. Subhadra was such an innocent girl and Arjuna felt a little bad about the whole story now. He hesitated for a second, then, continued, "Yes, I was too afraid and I waited many years before I made up my mind to tell her. I knew that just like in all things in life, there is a time for you to speak, you have to be at the right place at the right time and do it when you have the chance. Because of the delay, her marriage was fixed with one of the kings our rival kingdoms and she got married soon after that. I didn't do anything about it. I lost her forever." Arjuna hung his head as if it still hurt him today.

He raised his head after a minute. "You know, the funny thing is she didn't even know that I loved her," he said. "So, it's not her fault, never was. I didn't talk to her and I faced the consequences. After that, I went into a low phase in my life, sad and depressed. I kept thinking about her for a long time. I dint know what to do. I was wasting my life, but then just like you; I met a Swamiji from the Himalayas, a Lord Shiva devotee. He talked to me about spirituality and told me that he had been meditating since many years and that he had achieved enlightenment and peace. He helped me see how meditation had helped him stay away from the distractions of the world. I became convinced that if the Lord was impressed one would be able to ask for anything from Him."

Arjuna was coming to the end of his long tale. "That's why I decided to renounce my life and go to the mountains," he sighed. "It was the only way to survive. This way, if the Lord liked me, he would offer me a boon. I would just forget my old life and start a fresh one."

A few seconds of silence. Then Subhadra asked, "Did you see the Lord and attain enlightenment? Did you ask for a boon?"

"No, I did not" he said. "So, I have decided that after this break of mine, I will go to the Himalayas and won't stop meditating till I see Lord Shiva."

He was good at making up stories and he had escaped from many difficult situations like these before. Draupadi and him had managed to sneak around during the first two years after her marriage to the five Pandavas. The first two years which were considered to be the most romantic and best years of marriage, Draupadi had spent time almost entirely with Arjuna. The other brothers were too busy with the rebuilding of Indraprastha to see through their stories. Arjuna knew it was unfair to them because in the end, all five Pandavas got equal credit for Indraprastha. So, Arjuna got the best of both worlds. But he consoled himself with the thought that it was he who had won Draupadi at the swayamvar.

"Can I ask you a personal question?" Subhadra interrupted Arjuna's thoughts.

Arjuna smiled and replied, "There is nothing personal in the life of a hermit. Please go ahead."

"Swamiji, what are you going to ask for when you get a wish from Lord Shiva? Are you going to ask the Lord to bring the woman back to your life? Are you going to ask Him to give you one more chance at your love?"

Arjuna thought about it. He said, "I have to be honest, the main reason I went to meditate was to forget her, but now I don't think I will go back to my normal life again. I love what I am doing. But yes, that is the only regret I have in life...not telling her how I feel...if I get a wish I will ask the Lord to give all men like me who are not able to express their emotions the strength to speak freely to their lovers and unite with them. From now on, that is my goal, to unite people. To spread love in the world."

Subhadra was expecting an answer like that, and Arjuna knew what she wanted to hear. He wanted Subhadra to know how far he was ready to go to love someone. He wanted her to respect him for that. She was lost in the story and little did she know that the man before her was making all this up just to impress her.

"We have spoken for a long time," Arjuna said. "I do hope that the lessons I learnt help you in your life. Always follow your heart. And remember, if you find a person who loves you more than you love him, then he is the right man for you. Say yes to him. Don't even think twice about it."

'Yes, Swamiji," she said as she closed her eyes and prayed.

"Okay, let's meditate for some time. After that you are free to go," he said.

Subhadra followed his instruction and started meditating. Arjuna closed his eyes and thought about what he had said to her. He hoped that this conversation had made a positive impact on her. They continued till noon and then said goodbye. Subhadra went back to her house which was located adjacent to the place where he was staying

Arjuna settled down in his room and ate some fruits. He wasn't all that hungry. All he wanted was to sit back and relax for a while.

37

The Best Yoga Session

The next day, again, Subhadra was right on time. Arjuna had woken up early that morning to get ready for their session. He opted for yoga this time because he thought it would be interesting and fun. He was looking forward to practising yoga with her. He gave her simple stretching exercises that he had picked up from his training days: touch your toes, do some abdominal exercises, lift your legs, do modified crunches. It was more like a workout than pure yoga. Arjuna was behaving like her personal trainer, but she didn't question his workout routine. She was a good student.

"Some stretching exercises are very good for the body," Arjuna reminded her. "Physical conditioning is as important for a person body as mental conditioning and meditation. So, try and keep yourself active all the time."

Of all the beautiful memories he carried with him of Subhadra and that yoga session, one stood out in his mind. Arjuna had asked her to do the surya namaskar, a modified version of it.

"Stretch your left leg in front like this," he said, stretching his leg forward and flexing it slightly to bend at his knee.

He couldn't stretch properly because he had not worked out since he left Manipur. He wasn't exactly in the best shape.

Subhadra followed his lead. She wore a light cream-coloured blouse, just a bit darker than her skin. Thin strips supported it, a thread tied it together at the back. Her back was completely bare. She wasn't wearing an angavastram this time; her toned abdomen was on display. Arjuna could clearly see her perfect hourglass figure. Her midriff was flat; her hips were curvaceous and wide. Her eyes were lined with green that day. Her hair was tied up. She wore a short dhoti that ended mid-thigh. She wanted to be free during the stretches and she seemed comfortable being around Arjuna. His tragic love story may have helped her feel safe around him. Women like men who have been in committed relationships because it shows that they can be faithful and passionate in love.

Arjuna stretched his arms, folded his palms in the namaste position, then, closed his eyes, took a deep breath and raised his hands forward and up in a swift, smooth motion. He stayed in that position for a few seconds and came back to the original standing position.

Now it was Subhadra's turn. She stretched her leg, the dhoti was restricting her, so, she pulled up the lower end of it slightly to let her legs stretch. She swung her leg a little, moving it up and down to make herself comfortable. As she flexed her leg, her thigh muscles became prominent. Arjuna couldn't help but steal a glance at them. She had long legs and her thighs were toned and smooth. Then, she raised her hands to do the surya namaskar. Arjuna was mesmerised by her movements. He remembered the first time he had seen Ulupi bathing in the river. The same rush of excitement swept him away when he gazed at Subhadra.

As she stretched her arms, the skin on her midriff got stretched and highlighted her ribs. Her abdomen was projecting out and her spine was beautifully curved inward in this pose. Her blouse which was exactly the right fit enhanced the shape of her body. She was already fully stretched, but she still pushed her limits. This showed she was willing to learn. She raised her head skyward and closed her eyes. She stayed in that position for a while.

Arjuna was very impressed by her beauty and endurance. He watched her like a man under a spell the whole time.

* * *

The yoga session was fun for both of them. The next day came the counselling session where Arjuna talked about his life experiences and his time with his fellow hermits. He also spoke about his past. Subhadra constantly questioned him about his love life and he answered her smartly, telling her what she wanted to hear. He made her feel the way he wanted her to feel. He had tried this the previous day and he knew she would relate to him emotionally if he built on it.

At one point, she told him, "I can relate to the girl you fell in love a lot, but I hope there is no one out there who loves me as much as you loved her."

"What would you have done if a man came to you and said that he loved you more than anything else in the world and wanted to marry you?" Arjuna asked her. This was what he wanted to know.

The question surprised her and she felt it was a real one. It took her some time to realise that it was a hypothetical situation. She replied, "I don't know, Swamiji. Right now, in my situation, it will be a difficult choice because my marriage is already fixed to someone. So, I don't see any reason to break my existing relationship."

Arjuna smilingly interrupted her. He wanted to convince her that this was the completely wrong thought process. "The reason, the one and only reason which you need to decide which man you want to spend the rest of your life with is his ability to love you. It looks like you don't have a lot of experience in this area, but you will understand as you get older," he said. "Child, maybe you don't want to break this marriage because it means going against the wishes of your brother, and going against society's norms. But it doesn't matter what they think, because you have to spend your life with the man, not them. People have been giving out the same old advice for long. I believe you should do what you want and not what society asks you to do. I learnt this the hard way by losing my love. It's not easy, it's not easy. Only the fearless are able to do it." Arjuna spoke in a very emotional tone to drive home his point.

Subhadra's thoughts may have been impacted, but Arjuna wasn't sure he had convinced her. This was going to be harder than he thought what with Balarama being eager to marry off Subhadra to another man and Subhadra's close bond with her brother. The one person who could help him out was none other than his mentor and friend, Krishna.

Two weeks went by and there were no signs of Krishna visiting Dwaraka or Subhadra's change of heart. Arjuna had heard from Subhadra that Krishna was supposed to visit them the previous week, but there was no news of him at all. Subhadra told him that Krishna's visits were mostly unpredictable; sometimes he would come on the expected date, at other times he did not arrive. He was a constant traveller and his plans kept changing.

38

Back to the Temple

Arjuna decided to continue trying his luck with Subhadra. He had two weeks left to finish his exile but he was certain he would be extending his exile atleast by a month or so till he could leave Dwaraka with Subhadra by his side. He had to spend more time with her to win her over. So, he decided to be with her in the afternoons as well. They had established a very good rapport with each other. Arjuna was careful not to maintain a guru-disciple distance between them. He tried to be as friendly as possible.

One day, he grew serious and said, "Subhadra, I have to tell you that I will be leaving very soon. It's time for me to go back to worshipping the Lord. I hope that I have helped you with some of my philosophy."

"Oh! That's so sad, Swamiji. I was starting to enjoy your sessions very much. And yes, I have learnt a lot from you," she replied.

"Good," he encouraged her. "People come and go. Nothing is permanent, change is inevitable. Always remember that. Always spend time with the people who love you, so that when they are gone you will have their memories to live with."

Subhadra nodded. It was supposed to be their meditation session, but they ended up talking at these sessions. Arjuna had noticed that it didn't irritate Subhadra and she enjoyed their chats.

"In my last days here, we will go outside, visit the temples, do some good for the people of Dwaraka every evening. We must make ourselves useful to others," Arjuna announced.

He had hoped that by saying that his time here was limited, he could force her to make a quick decision when he told her his real story. Maybe the urgency would help him. It was a gamble, but he would risk it.

"Yes, Swamiji. Let's do that. I am very happy to accompany you," Subhadra said in an excited tone.

Arjuna was happy that she had agreed to step out with him. The more time he spent with Subhadra, the better.

* * *

The next day, Arjuna and Subhadra went to the temple early in the evening during the peak hours when people visited the temple before going home to their families. First, they prayed before the deity and then went and sat near the statue of Lord Shiva. They did some meditation for a very short time. A small crowd had gathered around them. People recognised the hermit who had distributed food at the temple a while ago.

"Swamiji, should we distribute the food?" Subhadra asked. They had planned to hand out free food to the crowd, which consisted of adults and school-going children.

"Yes, please," Arjuna gave her permission.

Subhadra called out to her loyal helper, Padma, and told her to bring the food. Padma in turn passed the orders on to the men who were carrying the food. A group of around ten men came up to them with huge baskets and utensils filled with red sambhar, sweets and heaps of boiled rice. There was enough food to feed an army. People sat down in a circle to eat. The men started serving them.

First, some fresh mango pickle was served and it was an instant hit, the children licked it off their plates before the next dish was served. The pickle servers served them more of the stuff. Then came the rice and sambhar, freshly prepared and steaming hot. The service was very generous and everybody ate to their hearts' content. Some children were in such a hurry that they burnt their tongues as they pounced on the rice and sambhar.

Then Arjun asked the men and the servers to sit down and have their meal. He joined Subhadra in serving them their food. They were all big, muscular men. It was an easy task for them to finish off the food. Subhadra really enjoyed serving food to people. It was the first time she was doing this and though she had not prepared the food herself, she felt a sense of satisfaction to see everybody eating and having a good time. Padma and the men hesitated to be served by their mistress. They were embarrassed. It was unthinkable for them to be served by the person who had employed them.

Arjuna felt proud of Subhadra. She didn't hesitate one second to serve them.

"Padmaji, you have been taking care of me since the day I was born," Subhadra said, humbly. "I will never be grateful enough for all the sacrifices you have made for me. So, please let me serve you a little food."

The meal came to an end. Some of the children were still running around, thanks to the high energy the food had provided them. Subhadra's helpers had also finished eating and were disposing off the leftovers.

It was at this moment that someone called out to Arjuna, "Is there food for just one more person?" A familiar voice, Arjuna had heard it before.

Arjuna and Subhadra were on their way out, carrying the empty utensils and arranging them in stacks to make it easier for the men to take them back to the palace kitchens. Subhadra looked at her utensils and Arjuna's. There was still some food at the bottom. They could easily manage to serve one plate and if they scraped it together.

'Yes," Subhadra said. "Swamiji will serve you sambhar also."

She picked up a bucket of sambhar. Arjuna let her do it. He was tired and wanted to sit under the banyan tree to rest. Immediately, he heard a loud scream from Subhadra. He turned around. There stood none other than Krishna, smiling, with his arms outstretched. He had come visiting at last. Flushed with excitement, Subhadra kept the utensils on the ground and ran to her brother, jumped into his arms and hugged him tightly.

Krishna was thrilled. "It's good to see you, sister," he said.

"Yes, such a long time since I saw you last," Subhadra said as she pulled Krishna's right cheek. Though he was the elder brother, he wasn't very strict with her like Balarama. Krishna happened to be her favourite brother. Arjuna was happy that Krishna had come, but he was also very worried. There was a high chance of Krishna recognising him even if he was in disguise. Krishna didn't know why he was in

Dwaraka. He needed some time with Krishna to explain everything in detail.

"As usual, you never tell us when you are will be arriving, always you come when we least expect you. Why don't you want us to prepare anything for you?" Subhadra asked, holding on to Krishna. It was unlikely that she would let go of her brother anytime soon.

"I started from Indraprastha late, and I did take a lot of breaks during the journey" Krishna said. "Hence I got delayed a little, but I am here now and you know I don't plan anything in advance. I'm a spontaneous person." Krishna knew how much this irritated Subhadra.

Subhadra hit him on his shoulder, hard enough to hurt.

"What a pleasure to see you again. An unexpected visit like always," Balarama came up from behind and gave his brother a tight hug. Balarama was wearing his night attire, a lightweight, white, patterned angavastram and dhoti. It looked like a very comfortable costume.

This is the worst it can get, Arjuna thought. He had to escape from the scene without attracting attention to himself.

"Is there any food left for my brother?" Balarama asked the men.

"Yes," Subhadra replied. She spotted Arjuna hanging back in the background. "Swamiji, my brother Krishna is here, he would be delighted to meet you. Please come, Swamiji," she insisted.

Arjuna smiled nervously, "Yes, yes. It would be my pleasure."

Subhadra happily ran to her brother. "I have someone here I want you to meet," she said.

Arjuna stood at a safe distance from Krishna.

"Brother, this is my guru, my Swamiji who is a great devotee of Lord Shiva. He will be staying here in Dwaraka for a few days. He has been kind enough to share with me some of his vast spiritual knowledge. And this food distribution was started by him. He makes sure the people visiting the temple are fed daily," Subhadra introduced Arjuna with great pride.

Arjuna folded his hands in greeting. Krishna did the same but he was keenly observing Arjuna from head to toe. Arjuna looked away and wished he could disappear.

"Om Nama Shivaya, Swamiji, how is my sister doing? I hope she is not disturbing you too much," Balarama intervened.

"No, she is a very good student," Arjuna replied politely.

"Swamiji," Krishna stepped closer to Arjuna.

Arjuna stepped back a little, feeling uncomfortable.

"So, you are a devotee of Lord Shiva? How many years have you been meditating?" Krishna asked suspiciously. There was almost no sense of respect from Krishna when he asked the question. He never liked hermits or godmen.

Arjuna thought that Krishna would find out the truth about him. He took a few steps back. "I have been meditating for the past 15 years near the Himalayas," he said, ready to run in case Krishna caught him.

"I really respect people like you…renouncing the world and going to the mountains, surviving on basic food or no food at all. It's quite amazing. Every time I meet someone like you I realise how much more I need to know about life," Krishna said.

Arjuna was getting comfortable with the situation now. He saw Krishna was not suspicious of him. He was in the clear. Subhadra came back and stayed close to Krishna again. She was a touchy sister.

Krishna patted her head and continued, "Swamiji, I have never been the meditating type of person. I can't sit with my eyes closed for more than a few seconds. Actually I hardly sleep. So…"

"So, even you are going to join me from tomorrow," Subhadra intervened. She was impulsive in making suggestions. It was quite irritating for Arjuna and Krishna, but they let it go. Both of them loved her.

Krishna laughed. "We'll see," he said.

Arjuna smiled nervously. He didn't want Krishna in his meditation sessions; there was a high chance that he would make trouble for Arjuna there.

"Come, let me serve you some hot sambhar," Subhadra said.

"Subhadra, take the sambhar back to the palace. I can eat in peace there. I have much to say to you and Balarama. And you know I can just rest there afterwards," Krishna replied.

Subhadra ordered the men to take everything back to the palace.

Krishna turned to Arjuna before leaving. "I hope we can talk philosophy sometime before you leave," he said.

"Yes, surely," Arjuna smiled and nodded a few times as if he was looking forward to talking to him. He gave him a fake smile on purpose. He was frustrated with the situation. He needed to talk to Krishna in private before things got out of hand.

"Swamiji, aren't you coming with us?" Subhadra asked.

"No, I will meditate for a while here. You people carry on," he said. He didn't like Subhadra's enthusiasm. It annoyed him at the moment.

Balarama was standing at a distance talking to the head chef of the palace kitchen palace. He suggested some changes he wanted in the food being served. He wanted the chef to prepare larger quantities, not a lot of variety, just four or five items and one sweet. His aim was to serve more food so that he could feed everyone in the temple. This would definitely increase the number of visitors to the temple.

"Did you finish your meal?" Balarama asked Subhadra and Arjuna who were walking towards him.

"Let's go to the palace. We can eat with Krishna there," Subhadra said.

"What about Swamiji?" Balarama asked.

"He'll join us later," Subhadra answered, eager to meet Krishna again.

Arjuna watched them all leaving, unsure what to do next. He needed to talk to Krishna as soon as possible, time was running out. But he had to make sure to keep Subhadra out of it. That was going to be very difficult. He walked to the spot under the banyan tree. It was dark already. There was no one left at the temple. A stray dog which was always roaming around the city came and sat next to Arjuna. He ran his hands over the dog's body. It was his only friend at the moment.

39

A Night with Krishna

It was almost midnight now. Arjuna had fallen asleep under the tree. The moonlight was bright enough to light up the whole of Dwaraka, the temple had lighting as well. Arjuna was sleeping on his side, with his head and shoulders touching the ground, his tongue hanging out a little like the dog's, which was peacefully sleeping near his leg. This wasn't his usual sleeping position. He slept on his stomach but that he could do only on a bed and not on the hard ground.

His present position looked very uncomfortable as if he was partly sitting and partly lying down. It was like he had fallen on the ground from his sitting position, but he was fast asleep. Suddenly he was woken up by a voice. He looked around frantically, dazed and confused about where he was. He saw the temple and realised he had fallen asleep there while he was sitting under the tree and trying to rethink his strategy. He saw the dog sleeping next to him, with its tongue hanging out. He loved the dog. He softly stroked him.

"Well, that was some serious meditation you were doing! You are lucky no one has discovered the truth," said a voice from behind him.

Arjuna knew who it was. His secret was out.

Krishna was standing there. Alone. Angry.

Arjuna fumbled for words.

"How are you?" Krishna surprised him with a tight hug.

Arjuna was relieved. Krishna could never be angry with him. He was his teacher and everything Arjuna had learnt early in life, he had learnt from Krishna.

"It's nice to see you too," Arjuna said. He was breathing heavily. His body was still sluggish from sleep.

"I knew it was you," Krishna said. "Relax. Let's go sit over there. I haven't told anyone your secret," Krishna said, leading Arjuna to the temple steps.

He put his arms around Arjuna's shoulders. "You know I will recognise you anywhere," he said. "How can I not?"

Arjuna looked at him and both burst out laughing.

"Krishna, I am in a very confused and desperate state right now. I don't know what to do," Arjuna said.

"Yes, I am always there to help. Tell me all," Krishna said comfortingly.

"This exile has been very eventful," Arjuna said. "In this one year I have met people who I have made a part of my life. I have made them my family. And I don't know how to say this, but Krishna, your sister Subhadra…I have loved her since I first heard about her in my childhood."

Krishna smiled and looked up at the sky. "So, this is a love problem and it involves my sister?" he asked, his eyes twinkling.

Arjuna didn't say anything but the answer was yes.

"Well, I have to say, I have resolved a lot of conflicts and fights in the calmest way, but I am expecting this to be the worst of it all," Krishna said.

Arjuna waited for Krishna's promise to help him before saying more.

"I will take on this challenge," Krishna said in a minute. Arjuna knew his problem was solved. He grinned at Krishna and expressed his relief. "I travelled the length and breadth of the north this past year," he continued "And I don't want to lie to you. It was not as philosophical as I wanted it to be. I met two beautiful women who I fell in love with and we got married."

Krishna himself had many wives, so he understood Arjuna's feelings. They both easily fell in love and there was nothing wrong with marrying more than one woman if you loved all of them the same.

"Subhadra has been on my mind and in my heart for so many years, so, I decided to visit Dwaraka while I came close to the city during my journey," Arjuna said. "But I didn't want to enter this place as Arjuna so...it was easy to be disguised as a hermit what with my long hair and all." He stroked his beard and his rough hair. His fingers got stuck in one of his locks. His hair was a bird's nest.

Krishna nodded his head in agreement. "You do need a little bit of a makeover," he said.

"I came to Dwaraka and visited the temple as a hermit. I used this image to get close to your sister. I saw her and I fell in love with her again." Arjuna felt overwhelmed by the memory.

Krishna fidgeted. He felt a bit uncomfortable hearing this about his sister.

"Subhadra is the most beautiful woman I have ever seen," Arjuna went on. "I love her, I want her and I will take care of her for the rest of her life. I will do anything for her."

Krishna tried to calm him down. He understood how desperate this man was to marry his sister. He knew the feeling because he had experienced such passion before. Krishna had so much experience with women and love had made him do the impossible more than once. He understood women (or atleast some of them).

"Arjuna," Krishna smiled at him. "You are just like me, easily vulnerable to any beautiful woman you see. And I think it's our best quality. It drives us to do something which we would not have done otherwise. Why do you think all great men are romantics? Why do you think all of them have an unquenched desire for women?" Krishna paused. His philosophy was worth sharing. "It's been this way since the very beginning of our species, the thing which motivates man the most makes him do things beyond his ken, makes him fearless."

Krishna remembered the numerous women he had fallen in love with over the years.

"It's more than just sexual desire, I love Subhadra," Arjuna tried to create a good impression on Krishna.

"Arjuna, I know you are in love, but that love is a product of deep desire. I understand it. I am on your side and I will help you," Krishna promised.

Arjuna smiled. At last, he had an ally.

"But there is one huge problem which you are aware of," Krishna warned him. "Subhadra's marriage has been fixed. Do you know who the lucky man is?"

Arjuna shook his head. He expected it be a prince or warrior, but none as good as him.

"Duryodhana and the Kauravas have arranged her marriage. Karna and Balarama have no objections to it," Krishna said.

Arjuna couldn't believe it—Karna again! The two were destined to fight. They fought for Draupadi and even though Karna was able to perform the task, Arjuna had won (he was lucky). Now it was Subhadra they would be fighting for. Arjuna didn't see how he could win Subhadra as the marriage was already fixed and Subhadra had no objections to it. Arjuna had met his match. It was said that if anyone could ever defeat Arjuna in battle, it was Karna. If Karna had the power, Arjuna had Krishna by his side. Only destiny could tell who would prevail and who would perish.

"But how did Karna…" Arjuna wanted to find out the reason for this marriage, but he gave up. He exhaled loudly and rapidly. As soon as Karna came into the picture, anger gripped him tight.

"Listen, don't worry about Karna and Duryodhana, we can't change their minds. Our only hope will be Subhadra. Whatever we do, we do it to her," Krishna said.

"What do you mean?" Arjuna questioned him immediately.

"You have one more week till your exile gets over but you will stay here for a month longer," Krishna shared the plan with him. "Continue doing what you are doing now. Act like a Swamiji, but also try and convey your feelings to her. In the end, we will decide a day, the day we leave, that's when you will tell her the complete truth about yourself. Understood?"

Arjuna was fine with the plan, but Krishna knew it wasn't perfect. Subhadra was a woman who didn't fall in love easily. She needed a lot of time to get to know the person. Arjuna was in disguise and she wouldn't be comfortable accepting his proposal. They needed an alternative plan if they wanted to pull this off.

"If we have no other choice, we have to take her from here forcefully," Krishna shrugged.

"What? Are you telling me that you want me to kidnap your sister and take her with me to Indraprastha?" Arjuna's voice shattered the night's quiet.

Krishna thought about it once again. "Yes," he replied confidently. "Yes, Arjuna there is no other way. I know how much you desire my sister; I know you will be a better husband then Karna. I don't want my sister to go through all this, but sometimes it's about getting what you want, it doesn't matter if it's the right or wrong way. I have learnt from life that you must be willing to do whatever it takes. That simple! Be a good person but you know all good people finish last and we can't lose this battle against Duryodhana."

Krishna was very clear he didn't want Subhadra to be married to Karna under Duryodhana's control. So, he would go to any lengths to stop it. And yes, he wanted Arjuna to marry his sister.

Arjuna thought about it for a few minutes. He lacked Krishna's confidence.

"Arjuna, there isn't anything wrong with what you are going to do," Krishna assured him. "You are a Kshatriya, a warrior, and for people of your caste it is considered a great honour to take a girl with you. There is nothing to ponder over. You love her and I know she loves you. It's just a matter of time till you are united," Krishna continued, determined to persuade Arjuna. What alternative did Arjuna have?

"What about Balarama? Karna, Duryodhana and the Kauravas will declare war against us. What about the consequences of that?" Arjuna questioned him.

"Arjuna, don't worry about the things that are not going to happen," Krishna brushed it off. "In matters like these, the most important part is convincing yourself and being confident. I will take care of the people you just mentioned. Leave them to me. Know that this is a risk worth taking. Subhadra as your wife or Subhadra as Karna's wife...you decide."

Arjuna exhaled deeply and looked at the sky. The moon was at its brightest now and the sky was clear. "Okay, I think we can make this work as a team. I trust you," he agreed.

They sat under the banyan tree all night, making plans and going over the details of the task they had taken on. Now, there was no turning back. Arjuna had to be brave and confident and carry out Krishna's plan to perfection.

40

The Final Touches

Arjuna continued doing what he was doing at Dwaraka. He conducted yoga sessions and the evening outings with Subhadra. Things went smoothly. Subhadra was enjoying Arjuna's classes and their talks, but she didn't seem to show any signs of attraction to him. Every evening, Krishna joined the two of them at the temple and he would act as a wingman to Arjuna. He kept telling Subhadra how good Arjuna was at everything. He heaped praises on Arjuna and shared his tales of valour with great enthusiasm.

He also tried to plant some doubts in her mind about the impending marriage. "Subhadra, tell me the truth, how do you feel about your marriage with Karna?" he would ask from time to time, often hinting that Karna was not the right man for her.

Subhadra raised her eyebrows and looked at him in surprise. She was unaware of Krishna's plan for her. "I am fine with the marriage," she kept saying. "Why do you ask me this question?"

Krishna spelt it out for her one day. "Well, let me tell you that I am not completely satisfied with your marriage," he said. "Balarama has made all the arrangements and gone to a great deal of trouble...I know it's all good and you are okay with it, but as a brother, I just want you to be happy, that's all. If you are happy, then it's fine with me.

Subhadra was quiet for a few seconds. They were at the temple, serving people food. Arjuna was serving the row right in front of them. He could hear everything they said. Subhadra kept looking at the people around her. She spoke after a pause.

"I am happy with the marriage plans, but you know, I wish I was marrying someone I am in love with. I wish someone loved me too deeply. But I don't think I could have met any man by staying inside the house and being so protected all this while. I had plans, but life had different plans for me. It's the way it is. I have learnt to live with it, just like Swamiji," she said, looking at Arjuna.

Krishna was surprised at his sister being so philosophical. He suspected this was Arjuna's doing and he was happy about it. Arjuna came to them and offered them some sweets. Subhadra humbly declined, Krishna happily ate them.

"One should experience love at least once in one's lifetime," Krishna said.

"People don't get everything they want. I hope I get something out of my marriage even if I am not in love," Subhadra said, exhaling deeply. Her chest was heavy with all the sadness she felt. She tried to hide her grief from everyone.

Krishna knew how his sister felt. This was a difficult time for her, but she never complained about it. He pulled her close and hugged her. He hoped she would feel comforted by this.

Arjuna watched them from a distance. He didn't know what was happening between them, but he understood that Krishna was playing his part well.

* * *

Arjuna and Krishna discussed their final plans. It was decided that Arjuna and Subhadra would be leaving soon. Yes, Arjuna would tell Subhadra the next night what was on his mind. If she agreed, they would run away together. It not, he would have to kidnap her. Krishna would stick around for a couple of days. He had to keep control of Balarama. There would be a very delicate situation to handle after Subhadra was gone as Balarama was overly protective of his sister, and the marriage was slated to take place in one week's time. If she left with Arjuna, Balarama would have a big problem managing Karna. Krishna had to convince them all. It was impossible for any other man to do this, but for Krishna it was merely a difficult task.

"Arjuna, your departure is not going to be easy at all," Krishna warned. "Balarama has stepped up the guards around Subhadra's house and yours. I don't think they will let you leave the house by yourselves."

"Yes, I have scheduled a late night meditation session tomorrow," Arjuna said. "Subhadra readily agreed to it, but I doubt they will let us step out of the house."

"Just see if you can convince them by talking to them, if not, you know what to do." Krishna was confident Arjuna could beat at least five men in hand-to-hand combat.

"I think the number of guards has been increased. There is a guard stationed at every three metres around the compound."

"Then you have to beat them all," Krishna said. "That is the only way and I can't provide you the weaponry because all of it is in the palace. You'll have to use your strength and skills." Krishna knew that Arjuna would do anything for Subhadra. No matter how bad the situation, Arjuna would try his best. Krishna's concern was the aftermath of all of this, not Arjuna's success in combat.

Arjuna had grown physically weak over the past few days. He had suffered a mild fever the past week from which he had recovered. He wasn't in his perfect warrior-like shape. Even though he taught yoga to Subhadra, he hardly did any exercise. He watched her exercise, mesmerised by her charms. But he was willing to go to any lengths to make her his wife. Nothing could stop him from trying. Draupadi was a gift he had won. Ulupi was a delightful deal between two powerful clans. His marriage to Chitrangada was the act of a saviour. He loved all his wives. But, this affair with Subhadra was different. He was obsessed with her.

"What are you thinking about, Arjuna?" Krishna asked.

Arjuna came back to the present. "Yes, I will fight for her," he said.

"Okay then, I will arrange for some transport at the edge of the city for you," Krishna said. "I suggest you take one of the guard's horses till there."

Arjuna nodded. At this point of time he would nod at anything. There was too much he had to do and his emotions were running high. He knew that all this planning would go to waste; tomorrow's task would be based on pure guts and instinct.

"Arjuna, take her to Indraprastha," Krishna went on. "There will be a lot of repercussions for this. Maybe a war will break out between you and the Kauravas, but be strong and do what your heart tells you to do. The Kauravas and you were destined to battle to death. Live your life without thinking about them."

Arjuna knew this was valuable advice. His Kaurava brothers would never agree to anything good. They did not wish him or his brothers well. So, he could not worry about their reactions to his actions. Among all the Pandavas, Arjuna was the one who spent the most time with Duryodhana growing up. He knew they weren't all bad. It was just that the greed for the kingdom had split apart their families. Even though Arjuna wanted the brothers to unite, it was too late now, and a war was coming.

Krishna and Arjuna sat silently for some time. They watched the clear night sky with the full moon drifting in it as they prepared for what was to come. The stray dog was sleeping on its back next to Arjuna; the temple had become its home. The dog had its legs up in the air. The night was pleasantly cool and the dog seemed to like it. It looked much healthier than the state in which Arjuna had found it. Arjuna wrapped his angavastram around his neck.

Krishna had completely covered himself with a cotton cloth. They were calmed by the night's silence, a few crickets could be heard, nothing else. Arjuna and Krishna always stayed up late at night when they had to deal with a challenging task. It helped them feel less worried about the outcome. After a while, they stood up and hugged each other. Arjuna touched Krishna's feet and asked for his blessings. They would meet next in Indraprastha.

* * *

Arjuna slept for a few hours after Krishna left. He had cancelled the morning and the evening sessions, there was only one last late-night session left. He had to prepare for the evening. He didn't have any weapons but he found the wooden blowstick which he had made to fight the hunters. He also had some tranquilising seeds with him. But the stock would not be enough to put out all the guards.

The compound in which his house and Subhadra's place stood was heavily guarded. The men had swords and shields. He didn't know whether he could fight all of them. He could handle them one by one without alerting the others. A lot was going on in his mind. In the afternoon, he walked around the house to check his surroundings and made a mental note of all the structures around. They would be of use to him later. He ate a light meal, freshened up, settled into his chair and waited for Subhadra to arrive.

41

The Decisive Night

Finally, night fell. The city of Dwaraka had completely shut down. Only the guards roamed around the empty streets.

Arjuna heard Subhadra enter the house. He stood up.

Subhadra stood in front of him with a bright smile on her lips. Suddenly, all his focus was gone. How could he kidnap such a beautiful and innocent woman? She was looking her best that day, dressed in shades of orange. Her delicate blouse was bright orange and tied at the back. Her dhoti was a lighter orange and it reached her ankles. Her hair was wet and tied tightly back. Her face looked fresh and clean, she had just had a bath. She didn't wear accessories, which made her look even more beautiful. Arjuna noticed that the moonlight gave her body an ethereal glow. Slim waist, full hips, her figure was perfect and temptingly sensuous. There was a spring in her step because she was healthy and fit. With an innocent smile, she waited for her "Swamiji" to instruct her.

Arjuna looked at her and felt bad about what was going to happen to her. She didn't deserve it, did she? Until now, she had listened to her brother, to society, done what she was asked to do. Today Arjuna wasn't giving her a choice, he was going to get what he wanted whether she agreed to it or not. It was not ethical, but he had one thing, one crucial thing, in his favour. He loved her more than anyone else.

Arjuna and Subhadra stood apart. She was near the door and he was at the opposite end, near his chair. The moonlight was slanting through the open central area. It lit up most of the central courtyard and then streamed in towards Subhadra's end as if it was a spotlight focused on her. Arjuna's end was darker. Other than the moonlight, there were a few candles there, but he made it a point to keep the place dark enough. He didn't want to attract any attention by making it the brightest spot in that area. He had to do this quietly and cleanly, without causing a lot of damage to Dwaraka or its people.

"Swamiji, Om Nama Shivaya," Subhadra folded her palms and bent her head.

Arjuna walked towards her, slowly emerging from the darkness.

Subhadra sensed there was something wrong. She saw him standing in the light, his face was dead serious, his jaws clenched tightly, he wasn't the smiling Swamiji who had been with her for the last one-and-half months.

"Swamiji, what is it?" she asked. "Should we get started or is something bothering you?"

Arjuna stared at the floor. His voice was low when he spoke. "Don't call me Swamiji," he murmured. He was loud enough for Subhadra to hear him.

Subhadra did not understand. What did he mean by this? She looked at him hoping to glean his meaning.

"I have to tell you something," Arjuna said. The night was completely silent and his voice sounded louder than it was. "Subhadra, I am sorry for what I have done." Arjuna was almost in tears, he was not pretending anymore.

"Why, Swamiji? What happened? You have not hurt me in any way," Subhadra assured him. She had enjoyed her time with him. She had learnt a great deal and become a better person thanks to him. He had nothing to apologise for. She was truly grateful for his presence and it was kind of him to have agreed to give her lessons. She had no idea why he was speaking this way.

Arjuna could see her face clearly now that they stood next to each other. She looked so beautiful and sweet. He couldn't do it; he wasn't going to kidnap her. He decided to tell her the truth about him, confess his feelings for her and then ask for her forgiveness. He knew Krishna would be very disappointed with him. Till date, he had followed whatever Krishna had said and won many battles and got everything he wanted. Right now, he couldn't go along with Krishna's plan and kidnap Subhadra. He might find some courage later. He didn't know. He wasn't confident about himself and this had never happened to him. He left everything to fate now. He did not have the heart to take her away forcefully.

Arjuna confessed to her. "I am not the Swamiji you think I am, I am not your guru, and I am not some hermit who has meditated in the mountains my whole life. I didn't come to Dwaraka just by accident." He kept his voice steady even if he was trembling.

Subhadra took a step back as she listened to him. She was scared.

Arjuna looked up at her from the floor. "All of this," he pointed his at his beard, his hair, his clothes. "All of this is a disguise. I am not this man, this hermit."

Arjuna could see clearly that Subhadra's pupils were dilated. She had never doubted him before. There was a chance she would scream, but she also needed clear answers from him. He knew that she was fond of him. She would wait to hear the truth.

"Who are you?" Subhadra asked, shocked.

"I am Arjuna, one of the Panch Pandavas, the rulers of Indraprastha."

Subhadra took a step back, she even lost her balance. Arjuna made no effort to do anything because he knew she would object if he tried to help. It was better if he just told her everything she wanted to know.

He said, "Subhadra, please let me explain. You know I don't regret anything I have done so far because whatever I have done, I have done it for you." Arjuna spoke with conviction and hoped she would believe him. "Subhadra, I have fallen madly in love with you. The only reason I came to Dwaraka is for you. I dressed myself as a hermit and approached you; I got your brother's attention by the temple food donations and found a way to get closer to you. I am no Swami; I am just a prince who is in love. But I want to say that all that I have ever taught you, the yoga, the meditation, it was all from my heart. I never for one moment wanted to hurt you."

Subhadra was on the verge of tears. She rubbed her eyes with her hands and blinked back tears. But, she knew she couldn't hold on much longer.

"So, all the lessons, the stories about your love, it was all made up?" she asked him, teary-eyed.

Arjuna didn't reply.

Subhadra suddenly put her hands over her mouth and started crying, but luckily for Arjuna, she didn't make a noise.

"I might have lied but that story about the love of my life, it was you I was talking about," Arjuna said. "I don't want to end up like the man in the story, which is why I am telling you how I feel about you. I will always love you, no matter what happens today."

Subhadra was in pain and she was too upset to hear what he said. Tears rolled down her cheeks.

"Please," Arjuna begged her to stop crying. He wanted to comfort her but words escaped him as he helplessly watched her weep.

Subhadra's sobs lasted for a while. Her face was flushed and she looked exhausted. He had never seen her look so pained and it was torture for him to see her in this state. But he couldn't wait any longer, he had to move fast. He was losing precious time. Atleast, he could escape by himself if she wasn't prepared to go with him.

"Why didn't you tell me any of this?" Subhadra asked between her sobs. "Why hide the truth from me?"

"I don't know…I was afraid…of losing you. So, I just couldn't risk it," Arjuna looked away. He remembered Krishna's advice about women, try not to tell them anything directly, in situations like these, be dramatic, be apologetic, be emotional and accept everything that the woman says, right and wrong. Arjuna just pinched his eyes with his index finger and thumb. No tears, but he pinched them hard enough to make them appear red. He could never cry in front of others, but his feelings were real. Arjuna was not good at expressing his feelings even if he had three wives.

Arjuna looked at her with his tearless, red eyes. "I hope you understand and forgive me for what I have done," he said, genuinely apologetic now.

They stood silently there for a couple of minutes. They needed the silence to rein in their feelings and think about their next move. Arjuna had everything planned, Krishna was on his side, but he had to wait to hear what Subhadra would say. Would she understand him? Would she forgive?

"You know, I remember all the things you taught me, every word you said," Subhadra spoke up. "And there are some things that have impacted me a lot. I agree that it is better to have someone who loves me more than I love him."

Arjuna face brightened up. He held his breath and waited for her to say more.

"Maybe it is true that you love me more than I love you," she let out a deep breath. It looked like she was slowly recovering from the shock Arjuna had given her.

"The choices we have are: either I marry you or Karna does," Arjuna said.

Subhadra considered her options carefully. She was a mature woman who could make her own decisions about her future. "Arjuna, this is the first time I have been given a choice and the sad part is I don't have enough time to think about it," she said.

This was the first time she had called him by his name. He felt very happy to hear her say it. There was silence in the room again. Arjuna reached for his tranquilising-seed-filled wooden pipe, which he could use to make her fall unconscious. He wanted her to go with him, and he had made up his mind.

"I would have loved you more if you had been frank with me," she said as she struggled to come to a decision.

Be patient, be patient, Arjuna told himself. His tranquilising pipe was ready and waiting to be put to use in case things did not work out.

42

Subhadra's Choice

Subhadra closed her eyes; she was trying to make a decision, a life-changing one. After some time, she slowly opened her eyes and a smile bloomed on her lips. "Let me give you a chance," she said.

Arjuna jumped up in the air. "Thank you!" he said, out of breath with joy.

"Calm down, you may alert the neighbours," Subhadra said. She was the one leading the escape now.

Arjuna felt like the luckiest man on the planet. All of his worries had evaporated and she was his now. Some work hard had to be done to bring this to fruition, but he would do the impossible with her by his side.

"So, what do we do now?" Subhadra asked, peering at the door to see if anyone was around.

Arjuna thought about. He had planned only for the worst case scenario, and now that she had willingly agreed to go with him, he needed to come up with an escape plan. The guards certainly wouldn't allow Subhadra to step out of the compound. The two of them couldn't be spotted together. If they stayed here and tried to convince Balarama about this, he would refuse to break off her marriage to Karna. They had to leave now if they wanted to build a life together.

"I wasn't prepared for this. I was actually going to kidnap you," Arjuna confessed sheepishly.

"What?" Subhadra shouted, but immediately realised her voice was too loud. "What are you saying?" she whispered. "Did I hear that right? You were going to kidnap me? What were you thinking?"

"I don't know, Krishna told me to do it…you know… just in case…"

"Oh, my God, even my brother is involved in this? I can't believe it," she shook her head.

"It's just that we love you and we would do anything for you," Arjuna said.

"I can see that," Subhadra frowned. She wanted to be angry at him, but now wasn't the time.

Arjuna felt relieved. He had told her everything and she would forgive him. She understood him well.

"So, what do we do now?" he asked.

Subhadra folded her arms across her chest. She spoke after a thoughtful pause. "What have you got with you?" she asked.

Arjuna looked around the room, checked his dhoti and took out his pipe. "Just this pipe and a few tranquilising seeds," he said.

It was not much. She only had a small knife with her for protection, but she didn't want to hurt any of her soldiers with it. She thought about all the dangers: they had to escape from the soldiers outside their house and ride across the city without getting caught. The first thing she wanted Arjuna to do was to shave. There was no man in Dwaraka with such a big beard and it would raise suspicion immediately.

43

The Escape

He shaved his beard off. The he filled his pipe with all the tranquilising seeds in his stock and followed Subhadra out into the open lawn where they used to do yoga and meditation. They climbed up a tree and jumped on to a thin ledge. Subhadra was thin enough to walk sideways without falling off. Arjuna was struggling, but he maintained his balance.

Subhadra's plan was to reach a tiny platform on the wall from where Arjuna had to tranquilise the guards at the front door so they could escape that way. But the problem was that some of the guards were standing and some were walking round. Arjuna needed to time his shots to perfection.

She reached the platform first, he got there seconds later.

"Come on, be faster, you are the greatest warrior here," she teased him.

The platform was a tiny one with space for only one person to stand there. Subhadra let Arjuna stand there as he had to do the shooting. She moved to the edge and found her balance on the ledge. They stood very close to each other and Arjuna tried not be distracted by her proximity. He loved her fragrance and he breathed it in deeply. She was just as beautiful and exquisite as the moon drifting in the sky. Arjuna willed himself to focus on the guards. There were about three of them near the front door and they were standing close to each other. The man at the centre was standing exactly in front of the door. The other two walked around.

"Look at the two men who are moving. When they walk away, aim at them, that's your shot. You have to hit at least two of them when they reach the extreme ends," Subhadra whispered in his ear.

Arjuna was in heaven right now because the love of his life was helping him to escape from the city with her.

"The best option would be when they are at the extremes, hit the extremes first, then the centre," she said. He agreed with her.

There were guards on all four sides of the compound, and double the number the back end because there was a bigger wall there. Subhadra was right to choose the front end for their escape.

Arjuna took out his pipe, his were hands shaking and he tried to steady them.

"Slowly, calm down. There is no need to hurry. I am not going to run away, I am with you forever," Subhadra whispered.

Arjuna took a deep breath. He had enough seeds for felling two guards. The third, he would have to use his hands. He put the wooden pipe in his mouth, clenched it with his teeth, and stabilised it with his hands.

Subhadra moved away a little to provide him with more space.

He observed the movement pattern of the guards. The central one was still there; the other two guards were slowly approaching him. The guard on the right walked at a better pace than the one on the left, but they would reach the extremes at almost the same time. The one on the right got to his extreme first. The one on the left reached his extreme a few seconds later. But then he walked up to the guard at the centre and stood there talking to him.

So, Arjuna had to change his targets. He aimed at the guards at the centre. It was easy, but the problem would be that the guard on the right would notice the fallen guards from a distance and could alert the others. Arjuna had to take his shots, so he did. The shots were clean. The two targets slowly crumbled to the ground. Suddenly, Arjuna noticed Subhadra running along the ledge to the right end, balancing herself, and then jumping on the guard at the right extreme. She landed a perfect chop on his head and made him drop unconscious.

Arjuna was surprised. He had always thought her to be a delicate, soft woman. But this was a good surprise at the moment. He ran to the spot where Subhadra stood, undoing the guard's armour.

"Well, that was a good move," he said.

"Now you need to dress like one of the guards if you want to ride across the city unnoticed," she said, handing him the armour.

"And you?"

"You see that bag right there?" she pointed at a big brown bag next to one of the fallen guards. "You are going to carry me in that and escape. That is the weaponries bag used to transfer light weapons across town to the palace, so, no guard will try to stop you if have the armour and the bag. It's a free pass."

Arjuna put on the armour, slightly heavy but manageable. It had a golden huge logo at the middle with two arrows crossed over each other and a small image of Lord Shiva at the top. Arjuna opened the brown cloth bag, Subhadra crawled into it. He easily carried her and put the bag on the horse carrier. The carrier was a square-shaped wooden box attached to the seat of the rider. Subhadra had to compress her body a lot to fit in.

Arjuna rode as fast as he could. Many soldiers were patrolling the streets but not one asked them to stop. Arjuna reached the spot Krishna had told him about. The horse and the chariot were ready for them there. Krishna wanted them to have a comfortable journey to Indraprastha.

44

Back in Manipur

Ulupi had been waiting for a long time now. Their son, Iravan, was five years old and under the training of the Naga chiefs. He was of royal blood and they wanted him to be the best Naga in the land. According to Naga tradition, the young ones had to spend a certain amount of time away from their mothers to attain independence, the earlier the better. So Ulupi decided to let him be on his own for a few years.

Ulupi missed Arjuna more than ever. Her son had kept her busy for a few years, but now she wanted Arjuna back. She couldn't go to Indraprastha because Indraprastha didn't allow Nagas to enter their territory uninvited, and she wasn't sure if Arjuna had given his people the news about their marriage. Ulupi decided she would set out in search of her beloved. She followed his trail and as she neared the city of Manipur, she received news from the locals that the little King, the young Prince, was celebrating his third birthday. Ulupi decided to congratulate Chitrangada on the way. She deeply admired the Manipuri Queen. She was invited to the palace to meet Chitrangada.

"Welcome, it's an honour to have a Naga Princess in our kingdom" Chitrangada said as she welcomed Ulupi.

They settled down and food and refreshments were served.

'Well, what can I do for you?" Chitarangadha asked cheerfully.

Chitrangada had a total change in personality since Arjuna left. She was a much more relaxed and fun-loving person now. She regularly did her training, but her son occupied most of her time. Her work ethic was still intact. She was having the best time of her life and she considered her husband, Arjuna, responsible for her happiness since he had gifted her son and an heir to the kingdom.

"I have come to wish you and your son the best for the future," Ulupi said. "I am very happy for you. May Lord Naga bless your family."

Chitrangada smiled and bowed her head. "Thank you, Ulupi," she said.

"My son has gone for his training to the south and my husband left a few years back on his travels," Ulupi said. "I miss my husband and so, I decided to follow his trail. Is there any chance you remember anyone, any guest travelling through your kingdom a few years back?"

Chitrangada tried to think about the many events in the past. She had an eventful life.

"To be specific, four years back," Ulupi said. "I know it's a little too much to ask, you are the Queen and I am sure you would have a lot on your mind, but I think you would surely remember my husband if he had passed through. He is a special man, a Prince."

Chitrangada tried again to remember the last few years. They had not had a lot of visitors and the clue given by Ulupi wasn't enough to go on. All of their visitors since she got married had been either royal princes or kings. Manipur had formed a number of alliances in the last few years.

"We we have had a lot of princes here, but I don't remember your husband," she said.

Ulupi was disappointed.

Chitrangada's little son came running into the room and hugged Chitrangada's leg. The three-year-old Bhabruvahana had a small bow on his back and a pile of arrows. He had got them as a birthday gift from his grandfather, King Chitravahana, who had showered his grandson with many gifts and sweets. Chitrangada pulled him on to her lap and kissed his forehead and brushed his hair to one side. Bhabruvahana wore a golden silk dhoti. It looked expensive. He didn't have any other clothes on; the heat was too much for the boy. His small belly protruded as he sat on his mother's lap. He didn't sit quietly and was continuously fidgeting with his bow. He aimed it all around the room and targetted the chairs and the many antiques. It was difficult to contain him so Chitrangada let him go and play.

"That is a very beautiful and energetic boy you have there. He is going to be a great warrior just like his mother," Ulupi said. She was tempted to pull Bhabruvahana's soft cheeks and play with him.

"I am blessed by the gods who have bestowed me with such a beautiful child and a loving husband. I just wish he was with me here," Chitrangada said with a smile.

They were silent for a few seconds. Both were probably thinking about Arjuna, their lives had dramatically changed after meeting him. Arjuna may not have been affected so much, they were all part of his life, but none of them could stake a claim to his whole life.

"Well, I hope my husband was with me too," Ulupi sighed.

"Where is he now?"

"Don't really know. I was hoping you could lead me to his trail." Ulupi continued after a brief pause, "I had met him a few years back when he was travelling across the country. I saw him for the first time near the Ganges and fell in love with him at once. It took him some time to understand my feelings but soon we got married. He has not returned since."

"That is a lovely story," Chitrangada said, but suddenly something struck her. Her expression changed. A Prince who was on a journey a few years back along the banks of the Ganges. She could only think of one: Arjuna. "Your husband..?" she was afraid to complete her question. She knew who the man was.

"My husband is the Prince of Indraprastha. He is one of the Pandava brothers, the great Arjuna," Ulupi said proudly.

Chitrangada's world suddenly became dark. She fell back in her chair.

Ulupi rushed to her. "Are you okay?" she asked.

Chitrangada looked at Ulupi. "A young Prince had visited our kingdom a few years ago," she said. "He helped us in our time of difficulty and restored Manipur to its full glory. We soon fell in love with each other and my father let us get married. That Prince is the father of my son and..."

Ulupi took a few steps back and slowly retreated to her chair. She knew the rest of the story. They needed some time to come to terms with this situation. There was no rule that Arjuna had to marry one woman, but Ulupi and Chitrangada loved him so much that they had not considered the possibility that he would have someone else in his life. They were both deeply disappointed with Arjuna. They loved him, had married him, borne his children, and more importantly, had waited for him all this time. He seemed to have moved on in life.

"You know, he fell in love with both of us and he decided to marry both of us. It's not his fault," Chitrangada said after a long silence.

Ulupi who was much more attached to him and passionate about their life together didn't speak.

Chitrangada exhaled heavily. "I have learnt to live my life happily, no matter what. If we look at the bright side, Arjuna has given us everything we wanted, children, our kingdoms' future and love. So, we are still lucky to have him as our husband."

She was right in a lot of ways. Arjuna was one of the most desired men in the country. Kings and powerful rulers everywhere who wanted their names to be associated with the Pandavas usually brought him proposals. He was the most sought after Pandava. Chitrangada and Ulupi were lucky because Arjuna had spent time with them. He had not been with Draupadi for very long after they got married. He had cared for Chitrangada and Ulupi and given them children, something they had always wanted.

"It wasn't his fault that he married a beautiful person like you. I don't blame him," Ulupi finally said. "He fell in love with both of us. I am happy you are his wife and not someone else's. I feel good about sharing my husband with you."

Ulupi liked Chitrangada and they formed an immediate bond with each other. She felt like she had found a new sister in life.

"Yes, it makes me happy that Arjuna chose you for me to share things with," Chitrangada agreed.

"Well, he has good taste," Ulupi laughed.

Again, little Bhabruvahana came running into the room pointing his bow at the walls. He was apparently fighting the enemy army all by himself. He noticed Ulupi and suddenly stopped running. He was shy in front of strangers. Ulupi extended her arm to reach out to him, but he stood a few inches away. She waited for him to come closer.

"Go, go to her," Chitrangada encouraged him.

Bhabruvahana, on hearing his mother, moved slowly and went closer. Ulupi got hold of his waist and pulled him to her. He stared at her continuously like he would do with any other stranger, but he didn't resist. He felt some kind of connection with her. Ulupi placed him on her lap. She tried to make him comfortable. He didn't respond. Ulupi rubbed his head gently; he had long, wavy hair just like his father.

Chitrangada could see that Ulupi was missing her son. "I know you must be missing your little boy," she said. "I know how hard it is to be without your child even for a few days. I absolutely adore you for sending your boy to training, I know even my time will come and I hope to be as strong as you."

"You are a very strong woman. The strongest and the most independent I have seen so far and I have seen a lot of independent women in my life," Ulupi said as she rubbed Bhabruvahana's back. He seemed to be comfortable now on her lap. He started playing with his bow again. Ulupi smiled and shook her head before continuing, "Life is so unexpected and strange. I set out in search of Arjuna hoping to find him, but then, suddenly, I decided to wish you and congratulate you and now here we are like sisters with a common husband we both love."

Chitrangada nodded.

"I love your son like my own," Ulupi said as she kissed Bhabruvahana's head. He continued adjusting the string of his bow, which was hanging loose.

Both Ulupi and Chitrangada were trained fighters, both of them had dedicated their entire lives to protect their people, and so, they had a lot of common interests. They talked for a long time about their plans. It was almost evening when they decided to part.

"Well, all good things must come to an end, it was a pleasure and honour to meet you," Ulupi said as she was getting ready to leave.

Chitrangada didn't want her to leave, she loved her company.

Ulupi did not want to bother anyone. She was afraid she would get in the way of the birthday celebrations.

"You are not interrupting anything," Chitrangada said. "You are the cause of more celebration for us. So, stay with us. It will give me the pleasure of your company. And you can relax here for a while."

Ulupi thought about it. Her son wasn't at home and she missed him deeply. By going back home, she would make herself miserable and think about him more. The palace was run by her father and her brothers, and there was no problem in peacetime to take care of. Maybe staying in Manipur was a good idea for both of them. Ulupi could do as she pleased and Chitrangada could concentrate more on her kingdom, knowing that someone trustworthy would look after her child. Ulupi accepted the offer. They hugged each other tightly. Ulupi would stay in Manipur and train Bhabruvahana throughout his childhood. She would make him a great warrior before leaving.

45

The Final Year of Exile

Hands entwined behind his head, he relaxed under a huge mango tree. The summer was coming to an end. The sky was clear and blue. The air was fresh and cool. It was a perfect day. Arjuna and his brothers were on the thirteenth and the final year of their exile imposed after they had lost everything they owned in a gambling match with Duryodhana and the other Kauravas. It had all happened 12 years back, but Arjuna recalled it as the end of their exile was nearing.

He never understood why Yudhishthira and the Pandavas had risked their entire fortune by gambling. It all started when Duryodhana challenged Yudhishthira for a casual match. He had nothing to lose by playing, but as the game went on, the stakes rose. Duryodhana let Yudhishthira win the first few matches to tempt him to play more and he did. The one thing which the best gamblers know is when to call it a day. They stick to a fixed amount, and that's it, even if they are on a winning streak. But Yudhishthira wasn't in his senses; he had fallen prey to the game.

He put the palace, Indraprastha and Draupadi at stake. He didn't know what he was doing and at that point, none of the Pandavas objected. The consequences were a lot costlier than they expected. The Kauravas took everything from the Pandavas and sent them to a thirteen-year exile during which the Kauravas had absolute control over Indraprastha. They promised to return control to the Pandavas when they came back.

The Pandavas went to the forest to spend their exile. Subhadra accompanied Arjuna because she couldn't live for so long without him. Arjuna was reluctant to take her because it would be unfair to his brothers, none of the others wives were allowed to come. But they had no problem with it and so he went ahead.

For twelve years, the Pandavas lived in a hut in the forest. They were busy with their own work. Bhim with his training, Yudhishthira with the administration of the household, Nakul and Sahadev had started writing a book about their experience in the wild and their experience of losing everything. Arjuna trained a little, but he felt bored most of the time, so he decided to travel in the thirteenth year. Arjuna convinced his brothers about his trip. He wanted to go on a solo journey and they let him go. Arjuna loved travelling and after his self-imposed exile many years ago during which he had met his wives, he was determined to be alone this time.

He chose to travel south and to the middle of the country, the unexplored areas. This trip would help him learn more about the culture and the art forms of the people who lived there. Little did he know that this would lead to a special encounter with the beautiful dancer, Urvashi.

46

Urvashi

One day, Arjuna was walking in the forest when he heard distinct beats and the sound of a dancer's movements. The beautiful notes of a dancer in full flow. Arjuna was eager to see who this dancer was and he increased his pace. The beats grew stronger as he walked to the middle of the forest. He couldn't see anything through the trees and bushes, but he followed the noise. He walked and walked and finally spotted a temple. Inside its courtyard, a woman was dancing in front of a statue of Nataraja. She wore a light blue blouse and dhoti; her hair was let down all the way to her waist. She also wore thick, beaded, silver ankle bracelets which made a lot of noise as she moved.

She was poetry in motion. From her swift movements, expressions and her posture, Arjuna guessed she was doing Bharatnatyam. He approached her when she finally stopped her routine with a pose, her hands curved like a swan and meeting above her head, her face tilted sideways with a bright smile, her hips curved to one side and one leg crossed over the other. When she noticed him, she almost fell down in surprise.

"It's fine, I'm not a thief. You can relax," Arjuna raised his arms to show he didn't have any weapons with him.

She calmed down. Her breathing became even. Like all of the women he had encountered in his life, she too was very beautiful. She had a dancer's body, which was a thing of exquisite beauty. Her small, light blue blouse revealed her milky white skin. She had many piercings on her body; her whole ear lobe was covered with earrings. Her nose had one big hook in it. It suited her small face. She even had a small hook on her belly button. It caught his eye. Arjuna had never had seen it on a woman. Only a woman like Urvashi who was bold enough to showcase her body in public could do this.

Arjuna was unaware that he was staring at her belly button for too long. Urvashi noticed and immediately covered it with her hand. She wasn't very comfortable with him at the moment. They had just met!

"Yes, so who are you?" Urvashi asked as she stepped back.

He cleared his throat and continued, "I am Arjuna, one of the Panch Pandavas, the ruler of Indraprastha." Even though technically he wasn't the sole ruler, he had every right to show off his royal heritage. He was attracted to her and wanted to impress her right away. But he didn't have any intention getting involved with her except wanting to learn dance from her.

"What are you doing here in the middle of the forest?" she asked.

"I am eager to gain knowledge about various cultures and about the dance forms of people here. I like meeting artists like you," he said.

Urvashi was sitting on a ledge with her legs folded up to her chest, unhooking her bracelets. She was done with practice and ready to leave.

Arjuna continued, "I was wondering if I could learn something from you. The art of dance has mesmerised me for years and I would love to understand it."

Urvashi removed her right bracelet, placed it on the side and raised her head with her hands on her feet. She looked at him for a few seconds, then, leaned back with her hands on the edge of the ledge and her legs stretched out.

Her pose surprised Arjuna a little. Her hands were behind her body, resting on the ledge; her breasts pushed up and her cleavage deepened, her abdomen showed a fold just above her belly button. Her dhoti was slightly pulled up and her muscular thighs were exposed.

"What do you want to learn?" she asked.

"Maybe you could teach me the dance which you were practising just now."

Urvashi smiled and went back to removing her other bracelet. She asked, "Do you know how many years I have been practising right here? Dance is an art of expression through your body. Many years of divine commitment is what is required. How long have you been dancing?"

Arjuna shook his head.

"I have been at it for 22 years, practically all my life," she said. "And you want to learn it in…how much time do you have? Surely, you being a Pandava and a royal, don't have a lot of time for dancing?"

"I have a few months and I am totally dedicated to learning this wonderful art. I really want to," he said.

She liked his desperation and his commitment, and so, she decided to give him a try.

"There, it's not like archery or sword fighting; this is Bharatnatyam, a dance form which was performed by the gods. It is much older than your archery. Maybe I can give you a glimpse."

"Well, with all due respect, archery has been there for a long time too and it deserves to be included among all the other art forms," Arjuna defended it.

Urvashi went back to removing her accessories and was ready to leave. "I have to perform today evening in the King's palace," she said, looking away. "I will teach you the basics. We will start your training from tomorrow, same place, and same time."

Arjuna was delighted to hear this. Finally, he was going to learn how to dance. He had been a bad dancer all his life. "Yes, yes, I'll be here," he said.

"And I'm not doing this for free," she said, asking for a reward.

Arjuna nodded his head. He could always give her some gold.

47

The First Day of Practice

He reached the spot before time the next day and wasn't surprised when he found Urvashi already practising. He didn't want to interrupt her, so, he stood there quietly.

"Namaste," Arjuna said after she was done. He bowed before her respectfully.

"It's fine, there is no need for all this," she said. "Call me Urvashi, nothing else."

Arjuna didn't want to anger her, so he agreed. He would do whatever she said if he could be a better dancer in the end.

"Go and sit there," she said, in an authoritative tone.

He sat on the ledge waiting for his turn.

Urvashi practised her Bharatnatyam for a few more minutes. Arjuna couldn't take his eyes off her for one second. He noticed that she wore a light grey blouse with a white dhoti, her belly button hook was still there and her nose ring was shining. Her lips were coloured bright red and her cheek bones were more highlighted than yesterday. She had wound her hair around in a loose bun, with some strands hanging down from both sides, which she pushed behind her ears intermittently. The sunlight gave a lovely glow to her sweaty body. She dried herself and signalled at Arjuna to come closer.

Arjuna went running to her.

She demonstrated a squat to him and asked him to try it. "Okay, you seem to be very stiff. Let's start with the basics," she said. "Bend your knees slightly."

Arjuna couldn't bend properly, his knees were hurting.

Urvashi pushed him down forcefully and he finally squatted. "Now hold it like that," she said.

Arjuna couldn't, his legs started trembling.

"What kind of a warrior cannot squat for a few minutes? Today, you are going to do this till you get it right," she said and sat on the ledge, watching over her student.

48

Urvashi's Behaviour Changes

The next day, even if Arjuna was on time, his enthusiasm was diminished. It was much more complex than he had anticipated. Pain radiated all over his legs. Urvashi had finished her practice. She was wearing all pink that day.

"Let's start with some of the basic postures," she said as she came closer to him. "Look at me properly, a good learner is always a good observer."

Arjuna concentrated on her.

She squatted, angled her legs to the sides, slowly and swiftly, extended her right arm to the side with her middle finger flexed inwards and the other fingers pointed out. It was the perfect pose.

"Did you see that?" she said as she turned to Arjuna. "Look at my fingers and my back, straight"

Arjuna nodded. This was exactly what he wanted to learn. Urvashi then shifted her weight and extended her other arm. She repeated it many times and then, slowly she started moving forward, taking small steps with her knees bent. This was when Arjuna understood that Bharatnatyam demanded the dancer to keep herself bent always.

"Look at my head," she said while she was dancing. Her head kept turning to the side to which her hand was extended towards. It was perfect synchronisation.

Arjuna watched her eyes, hands, legs and hips. She was the best dancer he had seen in his whole life. She stopped and looked at Arjuna. He quickly stood in position. He bent his knees slightly, they were hurting, but it was easier today. He slowly extended his arms.

Urvashi shouted, "Don't be so stiff, try and relax your body."

He loosened up a little. Urvashi came to him and corrected his pose. His hand was too straight, she flexed his elbow slightly, and then, she did the same with his other hand. She made him squat a little more in the most uncomfortable position. She even ran her hands over his chest to correct his posture. Arjuna was a bit taken aback by this.

The next few days went the same way. Arjuna sensed Urvashi's intentions. She was physically attracted to him, and every day, she kept getting closer to him. He couldn't resist her for too long.

49

The Dance and the Curse

Arjuna was a fast learner. There was a lot of competition he had faced during his archery training, from both friends and rivals. In fact, they had started their training much before him, but he caught up with them in no time. The reason he was the best at what he did was because he wanted to be the best. It was his mindset: he was desperate to be great. Desperation always brought out the best in him. Even in dance, he not only learnt but mastered the basics in just a month. Urvashi was impressed and she went on to teach him more complicated steps.

Arjuna continued tolerating Urvashi's advances, but one day, she crossed the line. He had come before Urvashi to practise his steps. Arjuna had developed the perfect posture and the body of a dancer, he had become leaner and flexible, he was able to squat on his knees, extend his arms, and tap the floor with his feet in time with the beats. He had even got the hang of the head movements. For a bad dancer, he was happy with all the progress he had made.

Urvashi had advised him to understand and bring out his feminine side. It would definitely help him with emoting. Arjuna was much more feminine on the inside than he cared to reveal. When he tried to express it, the resulting expressions were hilarious. Once, when Arjuna was practising his steps, he felt someone hugging him from behind. The hug was too tight for him even to turn around, he didn't want to push away the person and hurt her. So, he just waited.

"Arjuna," she said, breathing heavily on his back. Her hands were wound around his belly.

"Urvashi, what are you doing?" Arjuna said as he tried to gently get her hands off. But she had a strong grip. She didn't let go.

"Don't...Arjuna...let me hold you," she said. It was like her whole energy was poured into that hug.

Arjuna didn't understand this, but he still had his hands on her arms. He didn't force her to let go. But he made himself very clear. Urvashi forcefully ran her hands over his body. He felt she was being too passionate. He was confused. He enjoyed it and he resisted it at the same time. Urvashi felt no resistance from him after a while. She was free to do anything she wanted. She kissed his back a few times. Arjuna was sweating from the practice but Urvashi didn't mind that.

She went on kissing his back and her hands were all over his body. She was so passionate that she scratched Arjuna's body more than once. His skin was covered with scratch marks. She started kissing his shoulders and the nape of his neck, then, she forced Arjuna to turn around. She applied so much force that he almost lost his balance. Urvashi didn't wait, she jumped on him. Arjuna had no other option but to hold her. She wrapped her hands around his neck and her thigh rested on his waist.

Arjuna thought about Subhadra and about his vow to not get involved with other women. Urvashi wanted him, and he had tried to resist her. Urvashi's hair was all over his face. She pressed against his body and whispered softly in his ears. Arjuna felt her soft breasts against his chest. Her perfume smelt divine. But it was also very strong and it suffocated him a little. He let go of his grip on her. Urvashi held his face and kissed him on the mouth. The kiss was long, passionate and one-sided. Urvashi didn't mind.

Arjuna tried to move away from her, but he wasn't expecting such force from her. She held on to him and he submitted for the time being. Urvashi kissed his face and neck, holding on to him tightly. Arjuna was in danger of surrendering to her seductive advances.

"Urvashi, this isn't right. Let it go," he said, softly.

"Arjuna, I know you love me, just let yourself free," she said, as she lay on his chest.

Arjuna was tired. It was mid-afternoon and the sun was exactly overhead. He was sweating profusely. He waited for Urvashi to let go. He had to use force; he shook his shoulder harder and shiugged her off. Urvashi was almost thrown back a few steps before she found her balance. Arjuna knew he had used more force than required, but he had reached the limits of his patience. He tightened his dhoti. She stared at him in disbelief. She was breathing heavily and shaking violently. Her emotions were running high.

Arjuna raised his arms. "I'm sorry about that," he apologised for pushing her.

Urvashi was still breathing heavily. Her lips had gone dry and brown, from red.

"What are you doing, Urvashi?" Arjuna asked.

"What do you mean? I love you and I want you. I can't believe that you are asking me this," Urvashi said in disgust.

Arjuna understood she had madly fallen in love with him, but the truth was he didn't want her. He was attracted to her, but he knew this would not lead to anything meaningful. He had learnt from his mistakes.

"What's wrong with this?" Urvashi asked. "We are two people in love. This is what we should do."

"No, this is not right. We aren't meant to be together," he said.

Urvashi couldn't believe what she was hearing. She wasn't used to being rejected. She got down on her knees. Arjuna was afraid she would do something violent.

"You are the only man I have wanted so much. I love you. Please…we can live a happy life," she begged him.

Arjuna didn't say anything. His silence was enough. Urvashi waited, then after a few seconds, she wiped her tears, cleaned her face on her sleeve. Her tears had stained her cheeks and her eyes were red from crying and rage. Her face hardened. The sudden change scared Arjuna.

"I really want you and I have begged you for it but if you still persist on rejecting me, you are making a huge mistake," she said. "You are never going to get a woman like me in your life. Remember that I am the most beautiful woman you will ever see. I can give a man all the pleasure he desires. You will never even want to look at any other woman ever, not even Draupadi."

She was right. She was the most beautiful and the best. Arjuna had to make a choice. As Arjuna stood there silently, Urvashi moved forward quickly and put her hands on his face. She was back to her pleading. "Please Arjuna," she said as she ran her hands all over his face.

Their lips were very close to each other and Urvashi was moving forward every second, tempting Arjuna, but he stood looking down.

"Please," she begged.

He had made up his mind. His answer was no. With every second, she was getting more restless and violent.

She held his face and tried to force him to look up, "Come on, give me an answer, I want to hear it. Come on." Suddenly, she pushed him away. She tied her hair back tightly and adjusted her blouse. "Okay, fine, you have made your decision," she said.

Arjuna had rejected her so that he wouldn't hurt her more in the future, but she had taken it the wrong way.

"Your insensitive reaction mocks my vulnerable feelings. You are nothing but a coward," she burst out. "You don't respect us and don't deserve the pleasure of a woman's company. I pray to God that you spend the next year in complete isolation without getting physical pleasure from any woman. You will live as a eunuch. You will have the most beautiful woman around you but you won't be able to touch them and make love to them. Only then will you understand my suffering. You will experience my pain and you will cry," she cursed him.

Arjuna had nothing to say, nothing to give. He decided to leave.

"I'm sorry," he said.

"You will be sorry for this, and one day you will cry and beg for me for mercy," she continued.

Arjuna walked away. His dance classes were over forever.

50

The After Effects of the War

The after effects of the Kurukshetra war lasted for a very long time. The Pandavas had never wanted the war to happen. They did not want to kill their brothers, the Kauravas. The war had eliminated all the Kauravas. The Pandavas had Hastinapur and Indraprastha under their control and they had formed good alliances with the majority of the north and the south kingdoms. They didn't have any major problems ahead of them. It was the start of peacetime.

Arjuna divided his time between Draupadi and Subhadra. His sons, Sutakarma and Abhinaya, were old enough to assist their father with war and administration. It was a good time for all, but they still missed their lost brothers. The Kauravas were a greedy lot, but the Pandavas and the Kauravas had grown up together. The time they had spent in peace was a memory worth cherishing.

The Kauravas had a bigger army and more wealth and strong warriors like Karna, but the Pandavas had Krishna by their side. Krishna was their chief advisor now. He had helped them win the war. The war was a consequence of the greed of the Kauravas. The Pandavas had come back from exile to Hastinapur hoping they would get back Indraprastha from the Kauravas. It was under the temporary control of the Kauravas during their absence. The Kauravas saw this as an opportunity to snatch away Indraprastha; so, they declined the Pandavas their rightful kingdom, which was now much bigger and richer than Hastinapur. Duryodhana wanted control over everything and the consequence was that Yudhishthira declared war against Duryodhana and the Kauravas.

With Duryodhana, Karna and Drona, the Kauravas had the upper hand but the Pandavas had the support of the people. The first five days of the war were intense. Arjuna and Bhim killed the majority of their opposition while Karna and Duryodhana went on a rampage. Both sides were tearing each other apart. The war could only be won by defeating the leader of the enemy camp. But before getting to Duryodhana who was in charge, Arjuna had to deal with Karna to ensure victory.

Karna was the only warrior who was considered to be stronger and better than Arjuna. The Kurukshetra war would become the most unfair battle between the two. They both fought fiercely with each other, arrows were fired from long distances, and both were head to head and remained a close match till the gods started favouring Arjuna. He couldn't have survived if the battle went on any longer. Karna who was blessed with celestial powers couldn't use them against Arjuna, his lightning-speed arrows weren't any use, all of his powers were neutralised by the gods.

Arjuna on the other hand was given extra energy, replenished every minute, he could fight forever. He didn't have any shortage of arrows; they kept coming back, bigger and better and faster. Karna didn't have his shield as he had given it to his tribe the previous day for their protection.

Nothing was going his way but he fought bravely and fearlessly. The battle lasted for two days before one of Arjuna's arrows pierced his heart. This was the first major victory for the Pandavas and a major blow to the Kauravas. The war was half won.

Karna's death shattered Duryodhana completely. He lost his friend, his brother, Karna. He had raised and trained with care Karna throughout his life. Duryodhana's anger at Arjuna and the Pandavas peaked and he stepped into the battlefield himself. He was a monster on the battlefield, killing anyone he spotted. His whole body was protected by his powerful shield and he couldn't be stopped. He was invincible.

Krishna knew it would be unwise of Arjuna to fight against Duryodhana. It would be a foolish decision because there was no way Arjuna could win defeat Duryodhana at the moment. Arjuna was not a good hand-to-hand fighter and his arrows just wouldn't pierce Duryodhana's shield. The best option against Duryodhana was Bhim. He was the only one who could handle Duryodhana.

He took on Duryodhana, armed with his gada. Krishna closely watched out for Duryodhana's weak spot, there had to be one. Bhim fought his best battle, but took a couple of big blows from Duryodhana. He was severely injured but he kept fighting. It looked like he would lose because no matter how much force he had in his strikes, they didn't affect Duryodhana even a little.

Krishna finally managed to find a way out. He called Bhim to his side and instructed him, "Target his thighs, that's the spot which is going to hurt him. That's the soft spot."

Krishna was right. The only spot where Duryodhana wasn't protected was near his thighs, because there was no chance that anybody would attack him there. Krishna asked Bhim to focus every shot on his thighs. According to the rules of the war, no could attack their opposition below the waist. It was considered wrong and unethical. But Krishna knew there was no direct path to winning, if you wanted to be the best you had to do what it takes.

Bhim was badly wounded but ready to fight. He took a few shots at Duryodhana before finally finding an opening and hitting his thighs. This made Duryodhana limp a little, his first signs of weakness. This gave Bhim the boost he needed. The fight was one-sided after that. Bhim repeatedly hit Duryodhana on his thighs. Limping and bruised, Duryodhana fought till his last breath. Finally, on the thirteenth day of the war, Bhim jumped up high in the air and launched his deadliest blow to Duruodhana's left thigh, felling him for good. This was the end of the war. The Kạuravas had lost their King and the battle was lost. The Pandavas got back what they deserved, but the Kauravas were no more.

51

The Ashwamedha Yagna

The rage of the conqueror had overcome the Pandavas. Acquiring and rebuilding became an obsession. And so, they decided to conduct the Aswamedha Yagna. The Pandavas had almost the whole of the north under their control, and the southern kingdoms were their partners. The unconquered northeast was where they let the horse loose to grab new territory during the Yagna.

Destiny had other plans for Arjuna. The horse passed through the Kingdom of Manipur and according to the rules, he had to fight for the kingdom. King Chitravahana was no more and Chitrangada's son, Bhabruvahana, was ruling over Manipur along with his mother. Arjuna had not seen Chitrangada in years and had he had never met his son. Arjuna didn't even remember that he had once visited Chitrangada. In fact, after the Kurukshetra war, the only thing on his mind was the memory of that battle and a mountain of regrets about the happenings during the war.

As per the ritual of the Yagna, he attacked Manipur which was ruled by his own son. The battle was hard-fought and Arjuna's army was winning easily, but then again, in war, you win only when the opposition kills the King. The land belongs to the victor then alone. And so, Arjuna fought Bhabruvahana, a fight between father and son, both of whom didn't know they were of the same blood.

This battle was considered by many to be the most foolish mistake made by Arjuna. He had good alliances with most of the north and the southern kingdoms. There was no need for him to conduct the Yagna and amass more territory. He could have simply called it off. The trouble was that Arjuna had spent many years administering his kingdom and he was hungry for the thrill of war and fighting. However, this battle was not turning out in his favour.

During the Kurukshetra war, Arjuna had used some deceptive tactics against Bhishma to win the battle. He used Shikandi as a cover when Bhishma attacked him and defeated Bhishma using unfair means. This hurt the entire Vasu community to which Bhishma belonged. The Vasus couldn't tolerate this unfair win; so, they cursed Arjuna that his death would come at the hands of his own son. That day had dawned and Arjuna lay lifeless on the ground.

* * *

Ulupi saw Bhabruvahana's face as she finished reciting the tales of his father. Bhabruvahana's smile was wiped out. He was in shock. He had killed his own father and he felt the pain his mother Chitrangada was going through. He had never seen his father before, but he had heard stories from his mother, he knew how much she loved him and how long had she been waiting for him to return.

Ulupi too had told him many tales about his father. She had taken care of him throughout his childhood. Both his mothers had loved him so much that he never felt the absence of his father. He kept busy, trained regularly and helped his mother with the administration of the kingdom. He took responsibility from a very young age and soon started fighting wars. He had already won two huge wars for his people. He was a much more focused and a better-trained person than his father.

Bhabruvahana covered his face with his hands and looked at the sky. Tears rolled down his face. Ulupi felt her son's anguish. She went to him and pulled him close. She could feel his tears falling on her chest. She let him cry for some time. Ulupi and Bhabruvahana walked to the rest of the group in a while. She let him go to his mother. They stared at Arjuna for a few more moments, memories of him racing through their minds. After all these years, they still loved him just as much as they had when they first met him. They wanted to experience their time together once again. It had been the best time of their lives. Arjuna had spent very little time with each of his wives but the love which they had experienced in that very short time was enough to last a lifetime.

The sun was setting and was half-way down the horizon. Ulupi faced the River Ganga and folded her palms in prayer. She hoped that the Ganga was satisfied with the tales recited by her. A bright light slowly emerged at the centre of the River. The light became brighter and brighter as it rose out of the surface of the water. The light was now floating in mid-air, as bright as the sun. It slowly came towards Ulupi and landed softly on her palms which she had extended. This magical phenomenon brought everyone to their feet.

Ulupi held the bright light, her fingers closed around it, and after a few seconds, she opened her fist. The light was gone, but there was a green, sparkling gem in her hands. It was the mritasanjeevani, the resurrection gem. It had the power to bring back Arjuna to life. To give the world a great warrior back. But more importantly, to bring back a husband and a father.

Ulupi didn't say a word. She slowly walked towards Arjuna's body. The rest followed her. Bhabruvahana stood where he was. Ulupi kneeled next to Arjuna's face, holding the green gem filled with a liquid in her hands. The mritasanjeeveni was made by the Nagas and it contained a liquid made from the antidote to all poisons. The liquid could resurrect any person but only a Naga was able to access it. Ulupi summoned the gem to help her out. Ulupi slowly poured the liquid from the gem into Arjuna's mouth.

Arjuna saw all his wives standing in front of him, looking at him with red, tear-filled eyes. They were thrilled to see him. He slowly tried to sit up and they helped him. He looked around, for the first time in his life; all of his wives were together. Despite their tears, they had happy smiles on their lips. He was delighted to see them too. He was alive because of them. They were his biggest assets.

He knew that the best thing he had in life was not his wealth or his archery skills. It was the love he had got from his wives that made him who he was. He was nothing without them. He loved them all, but this was nothing compared to how much they loved him. He was the luckiest man on earth. He made a promise to himself that he would spend a considerable amount of time with each of them and give them all his attention and love. They deserved it and from now on, all his wives would live with him.

He opened his arms out wide and they ventured into his embrace.

Acknowledgements

I am deeply grateful to my parents, Shruti S. Hegde and Y. Sanath Hegde for their unconditional love and blessings. My sister, Sakinya Hegde Alankar and brother-in-law, Amith Alankar have always been kind to me. I've confided in Sakinya at every step of my writing journey.

Special thanks to my agent, Suhail Mathur and his team at Book Bakers.

Thanks to my editor, Vineetha Mokkil for her patience and diligent work on this book. Many thanks to my publisher, Om Books International for taking on my novel and letting me share it with readers everywhere.